THE BEGINNING OF A BRAND-NEW SERIES
FROM HIGHLY ACCLAIMED MYSTERY WRITER

SIMON BRETT

"Mrs. Pargeter is no spinster from a small English village. She is a wily, earthy widow, more likely to pick a lock than knit baby clothes. . . . An entertaining debut!"

—*The Washington Post Book World*

"Playfully taut, with false clues galore. . . . Without excess archness or the slightest whiff of camp, he amusingly reanimates an old-fashioned Agatha Christie setup—thanks to sardonic updated details, streamlined narration, and the highly engaging Mrs. Pargeter."

—*Kirkus Reviews*

"*A Nice Class of Corpse* is a traditional British mystery, full of eccentric types and false leads . . . an amusing caper."
—Newgate Callendar, *The New York Times Book Review*

"Simon Brett is the best serial mystery writer now setting pen to paper."

—*Sun-Times* (Chicago)

P9-CIT-145

By the Same Author

QUANTITY SALES

Most Dell books are available at special quantity discounts when purchased in bulk by corporations, organizations, and special-interest groups. Custom imprinting or excerpting can also be done to fit special needs. For details write: Dell Publishing, 666 Fifth Avenue, New York, NY 10103. Attn.: Special Sales Department.

INDIVIDUAL SALES

Are there any Dell books you want but cannot find in your local stores? If so, you can order them directly from us. You can get any Dell book in print. Simply include the book's title, author, and ISBN number if you have it, along with a check or money order (no cash can be accepted) for the full retail price plus $1.50 to cover shipping and handling. Mail to: Dell Readers Service, P.O. Box 5057, Des Plaines, IL 60017.

A
NICE CLASS
OF
CORPSE

Simon Brett

A DELL BOOK

Published by
Dell Publishing
a division of
The Bantam Doubleday Dell Publishing Group, Inc.
666 Fifth Avenue
New York, New York 10103

Copyright © 1986 by Simon Brett

All rights reserved. No part of this book may be reproduced or
transmitted in any form or by any means, electronic or mechanical,
including photocopying, recording, or by any information storage
and retrieval system, without the written permission of the Pub-
lisher, except where permitted by law. For information address:
Charles Scribner's Sons, New York, New York.

The trademark Dell® is registered in the U.S. Patent
and Trademark Office.

ISBN: 0-440-20113-6

Reprinted by arrangement with Charles Scribner's Sons

Printed in the United States of America
Published simultaneously in Canada

November 1988

10 9 8 7 6 5 4 3 2 1

KRI

To Chris and Missy

1

4 MARCH—7:15 a.m.—*I have decided today that the only way to get out of my current difficulties is by murder. It is really rather a surprise that I had not come to this conclusion earlier, since it will so simply and immediately resolve the problems that have been aggravating me for some time.*

Having reached the age I now have, I know myself well enough to recognise that the crime will give me no moral qualms. And as for the other great traditional deterrent to murder, the fear of being caught, that again does not operate with me. Indeed, arrest and trial might add a welcome excitement to the few years, or possibly only months, that I have left.

2

The diarist lived in the Devereux Hotel, Littlehampton, whose sea-front position was, according to the brochure, "unrivalled." However, few brochures were ever sent out; the clientèle of the Devereux tended to arrive by personal recommendation. There were only eight guest rooms; each was occupied by a long-term resident. And when, as was inevitable given the average age of those residents, a room became vacant, the hotel's proprietress, Miss Naismith, an unnervingly refined lady in her early fifties, had no difficulty in finding a new occupant.

In the early days, she had advertised in *The Lady*, but word of mouth from the established residents and their friends soon made such expenditure unnecessary. Miss Naismith always had a waiting list of elderly people eager to replace those who had moved into nursing homes (or taken a more permanent form of departure from the hotel), and she enjoyed assessing the suitability of these candidates. She felt confident in her ability to ensure that every resident of the Devereux remained "a nice class of person."

But when Mrs. Pargeter arrived at the Devereux in the middle of the afternoon of the 4th of March, Miss Naismith wondered momentarily whether her judgement might for once have been at fault.

She should perhaps have insisted on an interview, rather than conducting the arrangements by letter. It had been unfortunate that the proprietress had not been present on the day when Mrs. Pargeter had inspected the premises. The new resident had, of course, impeccable references, but no reference can pin down that indefinable quality of class, and Mrs. Pargeter made no pretence of being the genuine article.

For a start, there was the time and manner of her arrival. Miss Naismith had firmly suggested in her letter that two-thirty p.m. was the ideal moment for Mrs. Pargeter to appear, so that she would have time to settle her belongings into her room before the ritual of meeting the other residents at the Devereux's four o'clock tea, served in the Seaview Lounge.

Mrs. Pargeter, however, had chosen to appear at a quarter to four, making no secret of the fact that she had, "on the spur of the moment," decided to stop for "a self-indulgent lunch" on the way. Miss Naismith, whose orderly mind was shocked by the concept of doing anything "on the spur of the moment," also rather beadily received the impression that Mrs. Pargeter's self-indulgence had extended to the wine list as well as the menu. There was no question that the new resident was drunk; but she was certainly more relaxed and cheerful than might be thought appropriate to someone entering the portals of the Devereux for the first time.

Then there was the manner of Mrs. Pargeter's arrival. Miss Naismith had no objections to wealth—indeed, it was an essential qualification for her guests—but she did have an in-built resistance to displays of wealth. And to her mind, the hiring of a chauffeur-driven limousine was such a display. So was the amount of patently genuine jewellery that Mrs. Pargeter wore over her silk print dress.

So, particularly, was the liberality with which Mrs. Pargeter tipped her chauffeur and—worse—the Devereux's porter-cum-barman-cum-handyman, Newth, who appeared on cue to remove the profusion of suitcases from the limousine's boot.

Oh dear. Miss Naismith was beginning seriously to wonder whether Mrs. Pargeter really did belong to the élite who could be described as "a nice class of person."

The subject of her anxiety, however, either did not notice it or was unworried by it. Mrs. Pargeter was a widow of sixty-seven, imperceptibly on the move from voluptuousness to stoutness. The golden hair, which, in an earlier existence unknown to Miss Naismith, had turned many heads, was now uniformly white, but the clear skin, which had also been the subject of much compliment, still glowed with health. The backs of Mrs. Pargeter's hands bore the tea-stain freckles of age, but her rounded legs, beneath their grey silk stockings, remained unmarked by veins. Mrs. Pargeter, it could not be denied, was a very well preserved lady.

As she concluded her lavish tipping of the chauffeur and waved the limousine away, Mrs. Pargeter looked towards the steel-grey line of the English Channel and took in a lungful of seaweed smell. She nodded approvingly. "Good. The air's wonderful here."

"Oh, certainly, Mrs. Pargeter," Miss Naismith agreed in a voice of daunting gentility. "One of my residents, a Brigadier Fulton, once said that every breath of this air added five minutes to his life."

"Very nicely put. I'll look forward to meeting Brigadier Fulton."

"I'm afraid that won't be possible." Miss Naismith coloured. "The Brigadier wasn't, er, with us very long."

"Oh?" Mrs. Pargeter cocked a quizzical eyebrow.

"He passed on," Miss Naismith explained hurriedly, vexed at having to spell it out.

"Ah."

Miss Naismith changed the subject determinedly. "I do hope you'll be very comfortable with us, Mrs. Pargeter. I am happy to say that here at the Devereux I have very few complaints. Many of my residents do stay for a very long time."

"Except for Brigadier Fulton."

Miss Naismith did not like the smile of mischief with which Mrs. Pargeter spoke; it did not augur well for their relationship. "I can assure you, Mrs. Pargeter, that the Brigadier's death was not caused by anything he contracted at the Devereux. Without informing me, he actually arrived here with a serious heart condition," she added, in a tone of righteous betrayal.

And indeed she had felt betrayed. One of the other qualifications for her residents, clearly spelt out in the rarely despatched brochure, was that they should be "active"; in other words, in good health. Though Miss Naismith offered service and care to her elderly residents, she was very insistent that what she ran was a Private Hotel. There were Homes for people who needed Homes; but within the confines of the Devereux, serious ill health could only be considered an unpardonable lapse of taste. And death was a social misdemeanour without parallel.

"Dear, oh dear. Some people just don't think, do they?" Once again Miss Naismith caught an unwelcome glint of humour in Mrs. Pargeter's eye as she spoke. "Still, you needn't worry about me on that score. I went to my chap in Harley Street last month. Had the complete MOT. 'Some parts a bit worn,' he said, as you'd expect in a machine of my age, but generally good for another twenty years."

"That is encouraging news." The glacially serene smile returned. "And to what would you attribute your good health, Mrs. Pargeter?" (The "what" was heavily aspirated. Miss Naismith always gave full value to any "h" following a "w.")

The new resident sighed. "Well, I suppose while Mr. Pargeter was alive I would have said, 'Regular servicing,' but I can't really use that joke now, can I?" She smiled sweetly at her landlady. "Just go and freshen up upstairs."

And she marched determinedly up the main staircase in the wake of Newth, who was carrying two more suitcases. Miss Naismith's smile remained frozen in position.

By five to four all of the other residents of the Devereux were gathered in the Seaview Lounge. The tables were laid with crisp white linen; they awaited only the arrival of the chambermaid-cum-waitress-cum-skivvy, Loxton, with her trolley, bearing its load of silver-plate tea services, each pot carefully prepared according to the unchanging specifications of its destined drinker.

There was a considerable degree of interior speculation about the new arrival, but the residents of the Devereux were all far too genteel to voice any of it.

In the bay window, Colonel Wicksteed peered out to sea through his binoculars. He stood resolutely upright, daring age to curve the line of his spine. By the Colonel's side, stacked into an armchair under a tartan rug, Mr. Dawlish vaguely followed his companion's gaze.

"Tanker, is she?" asked Mr. Dawlish.

"No question." There never was any question in Colonel Wicksteed's mind. When he pronounced a vessel to be a tanker, it was a tanker—even if subsequent evidence proved this not to be the case. Fortunately, in Mr. Dawlish he was blessed with the mildest of associates, into the cobwebs of whose mind the thought of disagreement never entered.

"One of the big jobs," the Colonel continued. "Liberian."

"Oh. Now where is Liberia?"

"East Africa."

Mr. Dawlish let out an inane chuckle. "Funny, isn't it, to think of that boat out there not so far away, full of people speaking Liberian."

"No, no, Dawlish. Wouldn't come from Liberia. Just a flag of convenience, you know."

"Ah. Yes." Mr. Dawlish nodded sagely, as if he did indeed know.

"Not even sure if Liberia does have its own language. No doubt a lot of tribal dialects. There are any number of them. Came across a good few while I was in Africa."

"Did you learn any?"

"Few words. Smattering."

"I mean, could you write a letter in them?"

"Hardly. Many of them don't have a written tradition, anyway. Just oral."

15

"Carried in the mouth, you mean?"

"Yes, Dawlish."

"Like teeth, eh?"

Colonel Wicksteed pursed his lips and once again raised the binoculars to his eyes.

At the other side of the lounge, Lady Ridgleigh, tall and bony, perched on a tall and bony chair like a vulture over her tea table. Strings of undoubtedly genuine pearls hung from the tendons of her neck; below them was a classic grey silk dress, here and there over-shiny from careless or excessive ironing.

She condescended a smile across to Mrs. Selsby, an even thinner old lady, who was propped up on a sofa in the posture of a folded garden chair and half-heartedly fingering a copy of *Country Life*.

"You'll find there's a very stimulating article in there, Mrs. Selsby, about the hare."

"The animal, you mean?"

"Yes, Mrs. Selsby. Most stimulating."

Lady Ridgleigh, feeling she had discharged a social duty, relapsed into silence, and Mrs. Selsby obediently turned to the magazine's contents page and, peering through thick glasses, attempted to track down the recommended article.

On another sofa, near the bar, Eulalie Vance sighed audibly over a pile of yellowing letters. Though she believed she still looked as sylph-like and alluring as she had in the last publicity photographs taken of her some fifteen years earlier, an outside observer would have seen a thickened face and neck, framed in coils of greying hair, which was gathered at the back into an elaborate system of combs. The outsider would also have observed a spreading body, ill-camouflaged by an Indian print dress and a confusion of shawls and scarves.

And, if the outsider were so reckless as to enquire the cause of the heavy sighs that racked Eulalie's frame, he would receive a long monologue on the subject of her past love affairs. The other residents, who had all, at one time or another, been incautious enough to make the enquiry, now kept their mouths resolutely shut. Miss Wardstone, a beady tortoise of a woman who sat nearby, did not disguise her contempt but greeted each deep sigh with a sniff of disapproval.

Sigh, sniff, sigh, sniff. The rhythm was as regular as the ticking of the grandfather clock over by the door.

On her own, looking as if she might at any moment sink under and be overwhelmed by the cushions of her armchair, slumped Mrs. Mendlingham. Her eyes were unfocused; she had increasing difficulty these days in bringing them to bear on the reality that surrounded her. And focusing her mind was an even greater problem.

Her cardigan was buttoned wrong, and she wore odd slippers.

Only the regular shallow rise and fall of her chest showed her to be alive.

As the grandfather clock whirred a deep breath prior to striking the hour, the door of the room was opened by Newth, who ushered in the tea trolley, propelled by Loxton.

"Ah," said Colonel Wicksteed, waggishly turning to focus his binoculars on the trolley (as he did every afternoon). "Tea."

"Tea," Mr. Dawlish agreed.

" 'Tea, although he's an Oriental,' " the Colonel continued, misquoting Chesterton (which he also did most afternoons), " 'is at least a gentleman.' "

He let out his customary bark of laughter, and Lady

17

Ridgleigh (as she usually did) vouchsafed the witticism a smile of acceptability.

Loxton moved the trolley round its unchanging circuit, delivering the correct trays to the residents. Earl Grey for Lady Ridgleigh, served first by unquestioned precedent; Lapsang for Miss Wardstone and Mrs. Selsby; peppermint tea for Eulalie Vance; weak Indian for Mrs. Mendlingham, who would have drunk anything put in front of her without noticing; strong Indian for Colonel Wicksteed; and the same for Mr. Dawlish, who was, as ever, happy to agree with the Colonel.

Loxton felt mildly disconcerted that Mrs. Pargeter had not come when she was meant to. Loxton liked to have everything prepared well in advance, and the uncertainty over the sort of tea that the newcomer might require was unsettling. She bent down to retrieve plates of scones and cakes from the lower deck of the trolley.

As she did so, she was unaware of Mr. Dawlish's admiring eyes watching the outline of her buttocks strain against the black material of her uniform. His eyes appeared habitually hooded, half-asleep, but they took in a great deal more than the other residents of the Devereux realised.

3

The door opened with a flourish, as Miss Naismith ushered in Mrs. Pargeter. Though direct staring at the newcomer would of course offend the canons of good behaviour, the other residents did show considerable covert interest in her arrival.

"Good afternoon. Let me introduce the latest addition to our little family." Miss Naismith was prone, in her public utterances, to a rather cloying whimsicality. Turning first, as was correct, to the gentlemen in the bay window, she began the round. "Colonel Wicksteed—Mrs. Pargeter."

"Enchanted." He shook her hand and the rigid back bent as though hinged. Miss Wardstone's reptile eyes flashed a look of what could almost have been jealousy at the newcomer.

"Mr. Dawlish—Mrs. Pargeter."

Dawlish rose from his chair to his full height (which wasn't very high) and clasped the heavily ringed hand. "Delighted to make your acquaintance. I do hope you'll be very happy here."

Then he bent down to retrieve his rug from the floor, contriving on his way up to sneak a covert glance at the pleasing roundness of Mrs. Pargeter's calves.

Miss Naismith moved on to the ladies. "Lady Ridgleigh . . ." A bony aristocratic hand was graciously proffered. "May I introduce Mrs. Pargeter?"

Lady Ridgleigh smiled the sort of smile she had seen the Queen use when greeting Commonwealth leaders.

"My husband knew a Pargeter in the Guards. Cedric Pargeter, I believe it was. I don't suppose, by any chance . . . ?"

"No, shouldn't think so."

Lady Ridgleigh's smile changed to the sort used by the Queen when being kept waiting by Commonwealth leaders. But she persevered.

"May have got the name wrong. Froggie was terrible with names. Perhaps it was a Cecil or a Cyril or . . ."

"It wouldn't matter. I've never known anyone who was in the Guards."

"Oh." This was said with satisfaction. Lady Ridgleigh lived in constant fear of being outranked by new arrivals at the Devereux. It was comforting to know that Mrs. Pargeter presented no such threat.

The Grand Tour continued. "And this is Eulalie Vance."

The actress looked up from her peppermint tea, waiting a half-second for Mrs. Pargeter to say, "Oh yes, of course, I know that name. Aren't you the Eulalie Vance who gave that wonderful performance in . . . ?"

But since no such words of recognition were forthcoming, Eulalie shook the new arrival's hand and comforted herself with the thought that here was someone who had not yet heard the secrets of her passionate past.

"Miss Wardstone, this is Mrs. Pargeter."

"How very nice to meet you." The tortoise face was bisected by the horizontal line of a smile, but the eyes still darted suspiciously.

"Mrs. Selsby . . . No, please don't get up."

But Miss Naismith's words were too late. The long bones unfolded as Mrs. Selsby levered herself from the sofa to a precariously upright position.

"No trouble," she said. "I'm quite safe, you know." But the trembling of her body and short-sighted blinking belied her words.

"Pleased to meet you." As she spoke, Mrs. Pargeter gently took hold of a thin elbow and lowered its owner back down. Through the wool of the cardigan it felt as if there was no skin, only bone. Around the thin neck, Mrs. Pargeter noticed, clung a double string of artificial pearls.

"And, er, this is Mrs. Mendlingham."

The washed-out eyes remained unfocused, fixed on nothingness in the middle of the room.

"Mrs. Mendlingham." Miss Naismith did not actually raise her voice, but she reinforced it with considerable emphasis.

The old eyes flickered with realisation, then with alarm. "Yes, of course. I was listening."

"I don't believe you've met Mrs. Pargeter."

Mrs. Mendlingham, suddenly cunning, misread the intonation of Miss Naismith's words. "Oh yes, of course I have."

She rose energetically from her armchair and shook the hand of a bewildered Mrs. Pargeter, who had never

21

seen her before. The old eyes looked at Miss Naismith, as if gauging the proprietress's reaction. But they seemed disappointed in what they saw, and again lost focus as Mrs. Mendlingham slumped back into her chair.

Miss Naismith lingered for a moment, discreetly but suspiciously sniffing. Mrs. Pargeter, too, thought that she could detect a slightly unwelcome smell.

But no comment was made. "Well, that's everyone," Miss Naismith announced. "I do hope you'll be happy with us. Now do tell Loxton how you like your tea."

The waitress came dutifully forward as her name was spoken.

"Oh, hello, love. Like my tea good and strong, thank you."

"Indian or China?"

Mrs. Pargeter looked bewildered. "Well, Indian, of course."

Lady Ridgleigh gave an inward smile, vestiges of which appeared on her lips. There was certainly going to be no social contest with Mrs. Pargeter. Indeed, Lady Ridgleigh might even find herself enjoying the rare pleasure of "slumming."

"Well, Mrs. Pargeter, do take a seat. I'm sure you're tired after your journey."

"No. Fine. Only come from London. And did stop for lunch on the way."

"I'm sure you could still do with putting your feet up, Mrs. Pargeter." Once again, without being raised in volume, Miss Naismith's voice took on a steely edge.

"Very well, then." Mrs. Pargeter flopped into a vacant armchair. "Oh, incidentally, everyone . . ."

Hands froze on teacups. Scones were suspended between plate and mouth. They were not used to this. Residents of the Devereux were not in the habit of addressing the room at large. It was acceptable for Miss Naismith to make general announcements; it was allowable for anyone to come in from outside and pass an undirected remark about the weather; but residents of the Devereux did not address "everyone" in this bald fashion.

Mrs. Pargeter continued, either impervious to or ignoring the reaction she had provoked. "Please don't call me Mrs. Pargeter. I've never been one for formality. Everyone always calls me by my Christian name. So please will you?"

"And what is your Christian name?" asked Miss Naismith with frigid deference. The answer to this question would have great significance. Within her mind she had two rigid lists of names: those that were socially acceptable; and those that transgressed that First Great Commandment of her life, "Thou shalt not be common."

"Melita," Mrs. Pargeter replied.

Miss Naismith was confused. Melita was such an unusual name that she had difficulty in deciding under which heading it should belong.

This confusion reflected a more general uncertainty in her reaction to Mrs. Pargeter. Her first instinct had been to classify the newcomer immediately as socially inferior. And yet, the longer she spent with her, the more difficult Miss Naismith found it to classify Mrs. Pargeter at all.

And the more she began to suspect, with a degree of foreboding, that there might be more to Mrs. Pargeter than met the eye.

4

By five to six Newth had changed from his white porter's jacket into the red one with rolled black lapels that he wore in his role as barman. The Schooner Bar was on the ground floor, the other side of the Entrance Hall from the Seaview Lounge. It also commanded a view over the greyness of the March sea.

Newth wiped down the veneered surface of the counter. Wiping it down had been his last action before lowering and locking the grille at lunchtime, but he knew how quickly dust could settle. Though only in his late forties, he had the bachelor fussiness of a much older man.

As he stretched to the far end of the counter, he felt a slight pain in his chest, and took a few deep breaths until it went away.

He reached under the bar for two sealed white plastic containers. From one he filled a dish with salted mixed nuts; from the other he filled a dish with stuffed green olives.

He looked at his watch. Two minutes to six. He withdrew a bunch of keys from his pocket; they were on a chain that was clipped to his belt. He found a small one and undid the padlock that held down the grille at the front of the bar. (Miss Naismith made a point of telling all her new residents that this grille was not for internal security. The very idea of such a thing would be an insult to the integrity of her guests and staff. No, it was a deterrent to burglary. There was, regrettably, "a very unfortunate element" in Littlehampton, and she did not wish to encourage their criminality by having strong drink readily accessible.)

Newth pushed up the grille, again feeling a slight pang in his chest. Then he switched on the lights behind the bar and turned to the entrance to greet the first arrival, who he knew would be Miss Naismith.

"Good evening, Newth."

It was one of the conventions of the Devereux that, although they all saw each other almost continuously, the day should be regularly punctuated by new greetings.

It was also a convention that the day should be punctuated by changes of clothes. Though few of the residents ever undertook a more strenuous expedition than a stroll along the Promenade, they usually changed before and after these outings. And, though "changing for dinner" did not go to the extent of evening dress, none of them would appear in the evening in the same clothes that they had worn all day. None of them, that is, except for Mrs. Mendlingham, who seemed to be drifting ever faster into a world of her

25

own, a world characterised by odd slippers, stained cardigans and inside-out dresses.

"Can I get you a Perrier water, Madam?"

"Thank you, Newth," said Miss Naismith, as she did at this time every evening.

And, as he did at this time every evening, Newth reached down under the counter for a green bottle, and from it filled a glass into which he had slipped two lumps of ice and a sliver of lemon. The pouring was done below the level of the counter, so that, if there had been anyone else present, they would not have observed that the bottle, rather than the bulb-like shape so heavily advertised by Perrier, demonstrated the squarer contours made popular by Gordon's Gin.

Newth passed across the glass of colourless fluid. It looked rather flat, as if the Perrier bottle had not been sealed as well as it should have been.

Miss Naismith, however did not complain, but downed the glass's contents with considerable speed. Then she placed the glass on the counter. "Goodness, I'm thirsty today."

Newth, without further prompting, reached for a bulbous green Perrier bottle and, holding it above the counter, poured from it into the empty glass. The contents fizzed and spat bubbles in the air. Miss Naismith picked up the glass and turned to the door to welcome Colonel Wicksteed and Mr. Dawlish, the one in a three-piece suit of mustardy tweed and the other in a charcoal-grey two-piece that gave him a clerical air.

"Good evening, Colonel. Good evening, Mr. Dawlish."

"Good evening, Miss Naismith."

"Good evening."

The Colonel reached to the counter and took a small handful of mixed nuts from the dish.

"Here I go gathering nuts in March." The Colonel made this pleasantry at six o'clock most evenings (though he did adjust it according to the relevant month).

Mr. Dawlish cackled dutifully, and Miss Naismith gave the smile of a Lady Mayoress being presented with a posy at a Primary School.

"What can I get for you, gentlemen?" asked Newth, maintaining the illusion that one or other of them might suddenly ask for something different.

Colonel Wicksteed and Mr. Dawlish continued the charade of choice by chewing their lips and puckering their eyes, before deciding on "a large Famous Grouse" and "a small dry sherry," as they had every other night of their residence at the Devereux Hotel.

"Well," ruminated the Colonel, after he had raised his glass to Miss Naismith, said "Cheers" and taken a long swallow, "I wonder if we will find our new arrival is a drinks-before-dinner person. . . ."

Not all the Devereux's residents visited the bar in the evenings. Miss Wardstone had never set foot in the room. All her life she had been a total abstainer (from everything, as far as anyone could tell). Lady Ridgleigh had used to come in every night for a "desperately dry Martini," but of recent months had discontinued the habit. Mrs. Selsby had been forbidden alcohol by her doctor, and Mrs. Mendlingham was so comatose most of the time that she frequently had to be reminded to come down from her room for dinner, let alone for a pre-prandial drink.

"Oh, I think we'll find Mrs. Pargeter *is*," Miss Naismith decided, without saying that she based this conclusion on the new resident's lunchtime indulgence.

"It might be rather amusing . . ." Mr. Dawlish's cracked voice hazarded ". . . to conjecture what sort of drink Mrs. Pargeter would select . . . if she were to prove to be a drinks-before-dinner person."

He lapsed into a satisfied silence, having started this conversational hare.

Colonel Wicksteed barked out a laugh. "Kind of parlour game, eh? Could be amusing, yes. What drink would you suggest for Mrs. Pargeter, Miss Naismith?"

The proprietress of the Devereux bit back rejoinders about brown ale or port-and-lemon; instead, piously, she said, "I'm not sure that it's quite the thing to make that kind of speculation about fellow residents."

The Colonel was instantly chastened and contrite, as if he had suggested the idea. "No. No. Quite. Of course not."

They were interrupted by the entrance of the object of their speculation, who arrived arm in arm with Eulalie Vance. For dinner Mrs. Pargeter had chosen a dress in a rather bright ("strident" was the word that came into Miss Naismith's mind) blue. With it she wore a whole new set of jewellery—ear-rings, necklace and bracelet, all featuring what were undoubtedly real sapphires. Miss Naismith, while of the opinion that the effect was excessive, could not help herself from being impressed. Once again, she encountered difficulty in categorising Mrs. Pargeter.

"Right," said the newcomer, placing a plump hand on the counter. "What are you all going to have?"

This was not right. For a start, Mrs. Pargeter had not obeyed the ritual of exchanging good-evenings. Then, the manner of her question seemed more appropriate to a public bar than the cocktail lounge atmosphere of the Devereux. Finally, there was the whole issue of offering to buy drinks. . . .

Miss Naismith felt that she would have to intervene. Smiling the sort of smile a Lady Mayoress might use when the child presenting the posy had trodden on her foot, she murmured, incisively gentle, "Oh, Mrs. Pargeter, of course you wouldn't know, but I'm afraid a custom has developed at the Devereux that all residents buy their own drinks. It is not that we wish to be in any way uncivil; just that with such a small group of people it can sometimes be difficult to work out the precise obligations of reciprocal entertainment."

She did not spell out the reason why this "custom" had evolved—namely, that Lady Ridgleigh had proved rather readier to accept drinks *from* others than to buy them *for* others. The situation had almost led to unpleasantness. There had been complaints. And Miss Naismith had had to dig into her considerable reserves of tact before arriving at the solution.

Mrs. Pargeter was undeterred. "Don't worry, love. My first night here, we'll make an exception. Now, what's everyone going to have?"

Miss Naismith was too shaken by being called "love" to offer any further resistance.

Mrs. Pargeter took the orders. Eulalie Vance wanted a white wine and soda, which she insisted on calling a "Spritzer."

"Miss Naismith?"

"Oh. Well, I do tend to drink Perrier water."

"But, come on, you'll have something stronger tonight. In celebration of my arrival at the Devereux."

Miss Naismith was not yet convinced that this *was* a cause for celebration, but did concede that she might have a small gin. Newth reached for a glass, which absent-mindedly he started to fill up from the Gordon's bottle.

"A *small* one, Newth." Miss Naismith's hiss suspended his hand in mid-pour. "With tonic, please."

Giving a little nod, he completed this unusual order.

Then he produced the "same again" for Colonel Wicksteed and Mr. Dawlish. "For you, Mrs. Pargeter?"

They were all silent, waiting to have their unspoken conjectures confirmed or rejected.

"A vodka Campari, please."

Miss Naismith was forced to admit that she would never have guessed that in a million years.

"And what about you?" Mrs. Pargeter continued. "You have one with me, Kevin?"

Miss Naismith was thunderstruck. It was bad enough for Mrs. Pargeter to offer a drink to one of the staff, but using his Christian name compounded the felony. Newth did not have a Christian name, except on official documents; so far as the Devereux was concerned, Newth always had been, and always would be, just "Newth." The double affront deprived Miss Naismith of the power of speech.

"That's very kind of you, Mrs. Pargeter," replied the barman. "I'll have a half of lager, thank you."

Oh dear, thought Miss Naismith. I may have to *do* something about Mrs. Pargeter.

5

The thought did not leave Miss Naismith during the evening. There was nothing specific she could fault in Mrs. Pargeter's behaviour at dinner or afterwards; it was the newcomer's *style* that grated on Miss Naismith's nerves.

Mrs. Pargeter was too relaxed. She didn't have the tentativeness—the deference even—appropriate to someone joining the select company at the Devereux for the first time. Rather than taking her cue from the others, she seemed determined to put the others at their ease. The fact that she was succeeding in this endeavour did not endear her to Miss Naismith. People should not, in the proprietress's view, just walk into the Devereux and feel at home. They should start with a becoming reticence and spend a few weeks adjusting to the rhythms of life in the hotel. Then perhaps it might be appsopriate for them to assert their own personalities.

Why, Miss Naismith recalled, even Lady Ridgleigh, used to a lifetime of command, had been subdued when she first arrived. It was only after a couple of months that she began to become peremptory.

But, even as she thought it, Miss Naismith knew the comparison was inappropriate. Mrs. Pargeter was not peremptory. She was not unpleasant, not difficult. She was just very much at her ease, and very nice to everyone.

Which made her that much more difficult to deal with.

Miss Naismith brooded on this new situation as she mounted the stairs to her flat, converted from the hotel's attic.

It was half-past ten. Days ended early at the Devereux. Loxton had dealt with the bedtime drinks orders, prepared the various trays of cocoa, Ovaltine, Milo and biscuits, and left the hotel for the small council house she shared with her invalid mother. Newth had provided Colonel Wicksteed with his nightcap of Famous Grouse, wiped down the counter and padlocked the grille of the bar. He would now be doing his round of locking up, before descending for the night to his bedsitter in the basement.

Miss Naismith poured herself a tumbler of neat gin and slumped onto her bed. She picked up the remote control of her television and switched on to the video channel. She had been rather looking forward to seeing what Newth had selected from the Video Library this time. He knew her tastes well by now, and the title on the cassette, *Confessions of a Swedish Schoolmistress*, did sound promising.

But it was some time before she could lose herself in

the locker-room lubricities of the film. Mrs. Pargeter was still on her mind.

If she were to remain at the Devereux, the new resident might have to make some adjustments.

On the floor below, in her room at the back, Mrs. Pargeter reflected that, if she were to remain at the Devereux, the hotel might have to make some adjustments.

But nothing was insuperable and she did not envisage major problems.

She dropped off to sleep, as always, cheerful and confident, though without the expectation of sleeping very well. The first night in a strange bed, she always found, tended to be a little restless and broken. But she accepted this fact philosophically. It took a lot to upset Mrs. Pargeter. . . .

As anticipated, she did wake a few times during the night. Once she was woken by the sound of a door opening. She was not yet sufficiently familiar with the layout of the hotel to know exactly where the door was, but it seemed to be on the floor below.

She lay in the darkness, aware of the unfamiliar, half-heard rhythm of the sea, then she heard the opening of another door, the flush of a lavatory and, subsequently, a slight commotion, perhaps a small cry, from somewhere below. She wondered, without much urgency, whether she ought to get out of bed to investigate the noise.

But it was followed by silence. Only the sea swished distantly.

Then, as she drifted back to sleep, she heard a door close somewhere in the Devereux Hotel.

Had Mrs. Pargeter been on the first-floor landing and

witnessed the causes of these half-heard sounds, she would have seen Mrs. Selsby emerge, blinking, from her bedroom at the front of the hotel and totter, as unsteady as if she were on stilts, towards the bathroom (a visit that these days she had to make more than once a night).

Then Mrs. Pargeter would have seen someone else appear on the landing. That person was the only one living in the Devereux Hotel who kept a diary.

Mrs. Pargeter would have heard the lavatory flush and seen Mrs. Selsby move unsteadily out of the bathroom and start back towards her bedroom.

Mrs. Pargeter would have seen the diarist suddenly move out of the shadows when Mrs. Selsby reached the top of the stairs.

She would have seen the diarist push hard, and seen Mrs. Selsby lift and launch forward over the staircase. She would have seen the thin old arms flailing, fragile as sugar-sticks, till the brittle body clattered to a halt in the Entrance Hall, its chicken neck snapped sideways, its thin-lipped mouth locked open and still.

But Mrs. Pargeter saw none of this.

Nor did the other residents of the Devereux Hotel.

Except for the murderer, who looked down with satisfaction at the crumpled body, and returned to finish writing up that day's diary entry.

6

5 MARCH—3:15 a.m.—*It is done. It was even easier than I anticipated—no resistance, no commotion. I had been prepared for the possibility of an imperfect job, perhaps just of an injury and a tedious wait until she died of pneumonia, but I feel as confident as anyone who has not examined the body closely can be, that it worked first time.*

The temptation to check that she was dead was strong, but I resisted it. There is no point in taking unnecessary risks. I am confident that I have achieved what I set out to do.

And how do I feel now that I am a murderer? Have I been struck down by guilt and remorse?

No. I feel the same as ever. A little angry with myself, perhaps, that I did not think to resort earlier to this way out of my difficulties. And very exhilarated at the ease with which I did it.

To sum up—murder is easy and murder is effective. And, if ever the need arose again, I would not hesitate to commit a second murder.

7

Newth was the first to rise at the Devereux. Though some of the residents woke early, as is common for people of their age, it was another of the hotel's unwritten rules that no one should leave his or her bedroom (except to go to the bathroom) until half-past seven. By that time Newth and Loxton would have done all that was necessary for the start of another smoothly running day. Miss Naismith did not like the stage-management of the Devereux to be observed, and new residents who wandered round the public rooms before seven-thirty were quickly discouraged from the practice.

Newth rose at six; Loxton arrived half an hour later. Newth checked the central heating boiler, switched off the burglar alarm, and then unlocked the back door of the hotel to admit Loxton. After that he opened the front doors of the hotel.

By the time he had returned to the kitchen, Loxton would already have got the kettle on for the first of the day's many pots of tea. Newth would sit and enjoy a cup, passing the occasional comment on the weather, while Loxton prepared the Devereux residents' breakfasts. Breakfast and tea were the only meals for which she was responsible; the alternating team of Mrs. Ayling and Mrs. Denyer, who were in charge of lunch and dinner, lived out and arrived at the hotel around eleven.

On the morning of the 5th of March, this pattern was disrupted.

Newth rose as usual at six and by quarter-past was shaved and dressed in his white porter's jacket. He had been in the army for some years and did not believe in wasting long on his appearance.

When he was ready, he went to check the central heating boiler.

It was in the basement utility room adjacent to his bedsitter, and was an old solid fuel system. Though gas would have been less messy and cheaper to run, Miss Naismith was disinclined to make the large investment of replacing the boiler. So long as it worked, and so long as Newth was happy to cope with the mess, she felt that she was saving money by keeping it. In her running of the hotel, Miss Naismith made a great many dubious economies. Though obsessed by money, she was always resistant to anything that involved a large capital outlay, whatever long-term savings it might produce.

Newth loved the old boiler and tended it with great sympathy. Every morning he raked it out, removed the night's accumulation of clinker, and put in more fuel.

He found the warmth and the pulse of life from within the old iron body reassuring.

He checked it as usual on the morning of the 5th of March, then went upstairs to switch off the burglar alarm and admit Loxton.

His next task was to open the hotel's main doors, so that the paper boy could bring in the day's regular order and place them on the Reception counter. (The residents got very upset if their papers were left outside to catch the dampness of the sea mist or, worse, were folded too many times to fit through the hotel's letter-box.)

But on the morning of the 5th of March Newth did not get as far as the front door. The sprawled debris of Mrs. Selsby stopped him in his tracks.

Showing no visible emotion, he went forward to check that she was dead. Even without his army training, he would have been left in no doubt. The old lady was cold and still.

He paused for a moment, but his decision was quickly made. Loxton was unlikely to emerge from the kitchen, so he need not worry about her. Stepping over the inert form of Mrs. Selsby, he went quickly but silently up the stairs to the top of the hotel and tapped on Miss Naismith's door.

She was still asleep, but woke quickly, threw a housecoat over her surprisingly flimsy nightdress and came to the door. Newth explained the situation in few words and Miss Naismith instantly followed him downstairs.

She looked at the body in the Entrance Hall, then checked her watch.

"Put her in the Television Room, Newth. We don't want the other residents upset. I'll ring Dr. Ashington."

She went into the Office while Newth unquestioningly obeyed her orders. If he felt any distaste or perturbation at handling the corpse, he did not show it. Mrs. Selsby's body was still limp, though a slight stiffening around the jaw accentuated the strange angle at which her neck hung. With one arm cradling her back and another under her knees, Newth was surprised at how light she was. The skin had faded down to the bone, and now that too felt as if it might slowly dwindle and disappear.

Perhaps that was why Newth was so little moved. For a long time Mrs. Selsby had been like an old poster pasted to the sea wall, slowly washed colourless and transparent by the elements. Her death, the moment when the last outline could no longer be traced, had been part of a long, almost imperceptible process.

Dr. Ashington was not best pleased at being woken before seven, but when he heard that his caller was Miss Naismith, he became all charm. The proprietress of the Devereux unfailingly recommended him to her residents, and, since snobbery (if not wealth) dictated that most of them should be private patients, he benefited from the connection. Some, when they arrived, swore by distant doctors (like Mrs. Pargeter's "chap in Harley Street"), but most soon came to realise the advantages of a local service. And, since Miss Naismith's ground-rules for the Devereux excluded the chronically sick, Dr. Ashington's part of the bargain was not too onerous.

When he heard of Mrs. Selsby's death, he said he would be round straight away. "Is she still lying where she was?" he asked.

"Good heavens, no. I have the other residents to think of."

"Hmm. She shouldn't really have been moved. In the case of a violent death . . ."

"Oh, really, Doctor. What harm could it possibly do? She was definitely dead."

"It's not that. It's the kind of question that might be asked at the inquest."

"Inquest? Will there have to be an inquest?"

"Oh, I would imagine so."

Miss Naismith was very put out. She had not considered the possibility of an inquest.

But through the gloom cast by that thought glowed a little spark of excitement. Mrs. Selsby's sea-front room was one of the most coveted in the hotel. Miss Wardstone was top of the list to take it over, and Miss Naismith thought that the necessary changeover would be a good opportunity to raise the room's price.

And of course a new resident would have to be chosen to go into Miss Wardstone's room. Miss Naismith determined to make her selection with rather more care than she had shown in admitting Mrs. Pargeter.

And she also determined to charge rather more than hitherto for Miss Wardstone's vacant room.

Which was one of the reasons for the smile of satisfaction with which she replaced the receiver on the telephone.

8

By the time the residents of the Devereux descended for breakfast at about eight o'clock, Dr. Ashington had arrived, examined the corpse, and left.

Death, he had quickly concluded, had been caused by asphyxia following a broken neck. Given Mrs. Selsby's extreme frailty and short sight, he was unsurprised by her falling down the stairs. However, to Miss Naismith's continuing pique, he still thought there would have to be an inquest.

The Television Room was then locked, not to be opened again until the body was collected later in the morning by the local undertakers (jolly, thriving men who knew they were on to a good thing operating on the South Coast). None of the residents would notice the locking of the door, as the room was not used at that time in the morning. The watching of breakfast television (or indeed television at any time before seven-thirty in the evening—except of course when Wimbledon or snooker was on) was regarded as slightly *infra dig* at the Devereux (though Mr. Dawlish secretly watched TV-AM on a portable set in his bedroom, because he found himself strangely moved by the leotard of the Keep-Fit Lady).

Miss Naismith decided to delay the announcement of Mrs. Selsby's death until after breakfast. There seemed little point in putting the residents off their various orders of cornflakes, All-Bran, scrambled eggs, kippers and prunes. She swore Newth to silence and Loxton cooked away in the kitchen, unaware of the night's accident.

The other residents, all of whom appeared in the Admiral's Dining Room, did not comment on Mrs. Selsby's absence. It was assumed that she was having a tray in her room. This practice was allowed, though most of the residents, eager to stress to Miss Naismith how "active" they were, resorted to it infrequently. None of them wished even to hint at the social solecism of ill-health.

Colonel Wicksteed was always the first to finish breakfast. Although he ate more than any of the others, he shared Newth's military conviction that one should not spend too long on the indulgence of the body, and so wolfed down his scrambled eggs and four slices of toast and marmalade at great speed.

Then, wiping his mouth with a table napkin, he rose to his strictly vertical position, picked up *The Times*, which had lain correctly unread beside his plate while he ate, and announced to the company, "Well, time and tide wait for no man, so I think it's time I went to have a look at the tide."

Since he made this witticism almost every morning before a long visit to the lavatory and a brisk "constitutional" along the front, Miss Naismith knew that her cue to speak had come. She could not risk any of the residents being absent for the news and receiving their first information of the death from the arrival of the undertakers.

"Excuse me, I have an announcement to make." She gestured to still Loxton, who had moved forward to remove the Colonel's dirty plates, and Newth, who had just come in with a fresh pot of coffee.

"I very much regret to tell you that Mrs. Selsby suffered an unfortunate accident during the night. She fell down the main stairs and has, I am afraid, passed on." How bitterly Miss Naismith regretted that the English language did not possess an even more genteel euphemism for death.

The announcement prompted a ripple of reactions. Loxton let out a little scream; Mr. Dawlish, perversely, emitted a high-pitched giggle. Mrs. Mendlingham's vague eyes came suddenly into sharp, troubled focus, and she dropped the teacup that was half-way to her lips. Eulalie Vance, who somewhere in her much-vaunted past had been a Catholic, crossed herself instinctively; and on Miss Wardstone's taut face appeared, briefly, an expression of sheer triumph. Lady Ridgleigh's bony features set into the expression affected by the Queen at funerals of Commonwealth leaders, while Colonel Wicksteed said, "Oh, damned bad show."

Into Mrs. Pargeter's clear blue eyes came a new thoughtfulness.

And the diarist, who of course was one of those present in the Admiral's Dining Room, felt that really it had all gone off very well.

44

"I will be out for lunch, Miss Naismith."

"Oh?" The proprietress looked up from the desk in her Office, quickly forming the opinion that the red of Mrs. Pargeter's two-piece suit was, if not quite "strident," at least "bold." But once again the jewellery, yet another matching set, was real.

"Most of the residents do tend to take luncheon in the hotel, unless of course they are away visiting."

"Yes. Well, I dare say I'll take it plenty of times, but today I'm going out."

Miss Naismith couldn't be sure whether or not she detected a note of mockery in Mrs. Pargeter's echo of the word "take."

"That is all right, isn't it?"

"Of course, Mrs. Pargeter. So long as you inform the staff that you will not be taking luncheon before eleven o'clock in the morning."

"Which is exactly what I'm doing."

"Yes, Mrs. Pargeter. Though it is quite sufficient for you to inform the *staff*, as I say. Tell Newth or Loxton. There is no need to tell *me*. I often find myself very busy in the mornings. Particularly, of course, today, in view of the most unfortunate circumstances."

"Yes." Mrs. Pargeter paused. "Is the body still here?"

Miss Naismith winced at the indelicacy of such directness. "The undertakers have not as yet arrived, no."

"So where is it?"

This was really too much. "I really don't think it necessary for such details to be known, Mrs. Pargeter."

The new resident shrugged. "Very well. Please yourself."

Miss Naismith breathed deeply, then, with the strained smile of a lady at a tea party ignoring some-

45

thing a dog has done on the floor, asked, "And may I ask how you plan to spend your day, Mrs. Pargeter?"

"Thought I'd have a wander round. See the delights of Littlehampton. I don't know the town at all."

"It's not a large place. It won't take you long to see it all. I mean, there'd be plenty of time to see a bit, come back here for luncheon, and then continue your tour in the afternoon."

"Yes, I'm sure there would. But I just feel like going out for lunch today."

"Very well." Miss Naismith took in another deep breath. Mrs. Pargeter's decision upset her disproportionately. New guests should devote some time to studying the routines of the Devereux; once they had done that, then it was quite permissible for them to diverge from those routines, but not until after a few days' acclimatisation. Miss Naismith tried to find a way of expressing her disapproval, but all she could come up with was: "I'm afraid you may find the weather a little inclement."

"I'll survive." Mrs. Pargeter grinned. "See you."

Miss Naismith thought perhaps something really should be said. "I think you will find in time that the Devereux suits you very well, Mrs. Pargeter. I'm sure we'll soon get used to each other's little ways."

"Yes," said Mrs. Pargeter, pausing at the Office door. "I'm sure you will."

Mrs. Pargeter looked less perky as she ate her lunch. She had, as promised, examined the delights of Littlehampton, and found them much to her taste. It was a pleasingly tacky town. Mrs. Pargeter liked the evidence of new vulgarity slowly swamping a former gentility. Yes, she could happily live there.

But she did not smile as she sat over excellent fish and

chips in an empty riverside café looking out at the rushing brown water of the Arun estuary. There was something on her mind other than the suitability of her new home.

She could not forget the noises she had heard in the night at the Devereux.

She could not help speculating about the cause of Mrs. Selsby's death.

And she could not prevent those speculations moving inexorably to the conclusion that it had not been accidental.

9

Mrs. Pargeter returned to the Devereux for tea, arriving at almost exactly the same time as she had the day before. The afternoon was growing dark and bleak, with that peculiar melancholy of a seaside resort out of season. The wind swooped restlessly, setting up ripples of rattling among the shutters of the sea-front kiosks.

But Mrs. Pargeter did not feel cold. She had always been a good walker, and she had kept moving most of the time. Her calves ached a little from the exertion, but generally she felt pleased with her day. She had found her bearings in Littlehampton. She now knew where the Devereux stood in relation to the sort of services she was bound to need—newsagent, bank, chemist, hairdresser, public telephone, car rental agency, betting shop. Increasingly the conviction grew that she had found the right place—at least for the time being.

She was also increasingly intrigued by what she now thought of as Mrs. Selsby's murder. And she thought what an attractive project for an elderly person with time on her hands would be finding out who had committed that murder.

Loxton's memory for the minutiae of her job was excellent, and Mrs. Pargeter's tray arrived at her table with a pot of strong Indian tea. Mrs. Pargeter poured herself a cup in silence and listened to the conversations around her. She had decided that listening was going to be her most effective method of investigation.

"Sad business, sad business," observed Colonel Wicksteed, after a swallow of his own strong Indian brew.

"Yes, indeed. Will come to us all, though." Mr. Dawlish was suddenly and unaccountably struck by the humour of what he had said, and let out another of his manic giggles.

"Oh yes. 'Don't ask who the bell tolls for,' " the Colonel misquoted again. " 'It's for you.' "

"Is that a ketch?" asked Dawlish, abruptly pointing out to a smudge on the darkening sea.

Colonel Wicksteed's binoculars shot up to his eyes. It was too dark to distinguish anything through the bay window, but he pronounced with authority, "No, no. Some bloody *nouveau riche* gin-palace."

"Ah." Mr. Dawlish nodded, content with the answer.

"What is so *sad* . . ." Eulalie Vance dropped her voice thrillingly low on the word ". . . is that we could be the only people at the funeral."

"You don't know that," said Miss Wardstone combatively.

"Well, no one ever came to see her here, did they?"

"Doesn't necessarily mean she hadn't got anyone. Lots of people never visit their elderly relatives while they're alive and then turn up gushing tears at their funerals." Miss Wardstone spoke as bitterly as if she anticipated suffering in the same way herself, but since the spinster's customary manner was one of bitterness, Mrs. Pargeter did not allow herself to form any conclusions from this.

"Oh, I *know*. But it must be terrible to feel that no one cares. That's one of the advantages of living a full life, you know. Oh, there's pain and heartbreak, of course. . . . But I do like to think that when I die, there will be one or two people left in whom a little spark of memory still glows. That is," Eulalie added archly, "unless I live to a *very* great age."

Predictably, this was greeted by a sniff from Miss Wardstone. "Depends usually on whether the person who dies had any money or not. If they think they're in with a chance of inheriting something, it's surprising how many relatives suddenly come out of the skirting board."

"Well, Mrs. Selsby always gave the impression of being extremely . . . comfortable," observed Eulalie.

"Comfortable? She was loaded," Miss Wardstone snapped. "Her jewellery alone was worth more than most people's life savings."

The mention of jewellery brought both of them unconsciously to turn and look at the newest resident of the Devereux. Mrs. Pargeter studiously peered into her teacup.

Miss Wardstone realised she was staring and snapped her beady eyes away. "Oh well, it will be interesting to see who does inherit, won't it, Miss Vance?"

Yes, thought Mrs. Pargeter. It most certainly will.

"It is distressing," commented Lady Ridgleigh to no one in particular, "how much people are obsessed by money."

"Money does come in handy," said Mrs. Pargeter judiciously, looking across at the speaker. Lady Ridgleigh was wearing a silk dress in pale green and beige Paisley. Around her neck were the same strings of pearls, unsuitable with this ensemble, lost in the colours of the pattern.

"Oh, I agree one *needs* it, Mrs. Pargeter, but one ought not to have to *think* about it. That's why one employs little men like bankers and accountants."

"Yes. You certainly need someone around who's good with money."

"I suppose so." Lady Ridgleigh dismissed the idea airily. "Froggie—my husband—was not good with money."

"I was lucky. Mr. Pargeter was very good to me. Very generous."

Lady Ridgleigh was piqued by the implicit criticism. "It's not an issue of generosity. Froggie was extraordinarily generous. To a fault, perhaps. Generous to everyone. I suppose that's why he lost all our money."

"Couldn't you have stopped him?" asked Mrs. Pargeter, appalled at the idea.

"Good heavens, no. If a man can't lose his own money, what rights does he have?"

"But weren't you furious?"

"About the fact that he lost it? Good heavens, no. Mind you, the thought of some of the people he lost it *to* still rankles." Lady Ridgleigh turned her head graciously to look at Mrs. Pargeter. "Tell me, what was Mr. Pargeter's money *in*?"

Mrs. Pargeter coloured. "Oh, come, come, Lady Ridgleigh, you wouldn't answer if I asked you what Froggie's money was *in*, would you?"

"Of course I would. It was quite simple. His was in the family."

Mrs. Pargeter smiled. "Well, so's Mr. Pargeter's now."

At that moment there was a commotion in the Seaview Lounge. Mrs. Mendlingham had raised her teapot to pour another cup of tea and suddenly lost control of it. The pot had fallen, catching the edge of her tray, which was not centred on its table, and sending everything flying.

Mrs. Mendlingham rose to her feet, whimpering, though whether she was in pain from the hot tea that stained the front of her grubby skirt, or whether, as the wildness of her eyes suggested, some sudden memory had upset her, it was hard to tell.

Mrs. Pargeter went forward to take her arm, and was once again aware of the acrid smell that emanated from the old lady. This time there was no mistaking; it was stale urine.

"There. Are you all right?"

"Yes. Yes, I'm sorry." The wild, faded eyes tried to focus on Mrs. Pargeter's.

"What's the matter? What's upsetting you?"

"I just . . . I just remembered something."

"What was it?"

"Well, I saw . . ." But the confidence stopped short. A light of cunning came into the old eyes. "I'm sorry. My memory's not good these days. It comes and goes, you know."

"I think we all find that," said Mrs. Pargeter soothingly, trying to re-establish the confessional intimacy.

"But it seems to be getting worse. Sometimes I completely forget what I've done, can't remember if I've eaten meals or . . ."

"Don't worry about it. Worrying just makes it worse."

"I've tried all kinds of things to make it better. Trying to concentrate, talk to people about things. At one stage I tried just writing down everything that happened."

"A sort of diary?"

Mrs. Mendlingham nodded.

"That sounds a good idea. Do you still keep it?"

Again the shutter of cunning seemed to flick across the old eyes. "Oh, no. Not any more. I've given that up. It didn't work."

"I'm surprised. Still, never mind."

"No."

Mrs. Pargeter had by now manoeuvred the old lady back into her armchair. "Can you remember what it was that frightened you? Do you want to talk about it?"

The old head was shaken vigorously. "I can't remember. It comes and goes, the memory. Sometimes things are very clear, and sometimes I just can't remember what I've done. There are great big blanks in my life. Great . . . big . . . blanks." She lingered over the words, then, again suddenly devious, added, "Which is perhaps just as well."

Further conversation was halted by the majestic entry of Miss Naismith from the hall. "I heard a noise," she announced, and moved across to stand accusingly over the wreckage of Mrs. Mendlingham's tea.

"An unfortunate accident," said Mrs. Pargeter in a conciliatory tone.

"Yes," Miss Naismith agreed frostily.

Mrs. Mendlingham shrank into her armchair, avoiding the proprietress's eye.

Mrs. Pargeter continued to mediate. "Mrs. Mendlingham suddenly remembered something that upset her. You know, as she says, her memory is a little erratic."

"It is not!" Mrs. Mendlingham spoke with surprising venom. "I don't know what you're talking about, Mrs. Pargeter. There is absolutely nothing wrong with my memory." She rose out of her chair. "The reason for the accident was that the teapot handle was greasy. That is not the first time I have noticed a certain slapdashness in the washing-up in this establishment. I trust, Miss Naismith, that this situation will shortly be remedied."

Flinging this exit line behind her, she moved out of the Seaview Lounge with as much dignity as can be mustered by an elderly lady who has tea stains down the front of her skirt.

Her unexpected change of manner had the rare effect of striking Miss Naismith dumb.

And the proprietress of the Devereux was then presented with another bombshell.

"Well, I've done quite a lot of walking today," said Mrs. Pargeter. "I think I'll go up and have a bath now."

Miss Naismith rediscovered the power of speech. "Um, no, Mrs. Pargeter. Residents of the Devereux tend to have baths before breakfast or after dinner."

"Oh. Well, I tend to have baths when I feel like them."

An icicle formed on Miss Naismith's smile. "We all have to adjust our behaviour a little when we enter a new environment."

"Are you saying that there is no hot water at this time of day?"

Miss Naismith looked shocked. "No. Of course not.

The boiler is always on. There is constant hot water in the Devereux."

"Good," said Mrs. Pargeter. "Then I'll go and use some of it."

She had a good, long soak, continually topping the bath up with more hot water.

And, as she lay there, Mrs. Pargeter thought long and deeply about the late Mrs. Selsby.

And the still-living Mrs. Mendlingham.

10

An interesting conversation took place after dinner that night between Miss Wardstone and Miss Naismith.

Dinner itself was a formal affair, a kind of static square dance to which, Mrs. Pargeter recognised, there were fixed rules. That evening she was content to be an observer, not yet committing herself as to whether she intended to abide by those rules.

All of the residents sat at separate tables, except for Colonel Wicksteed and Mr. Dawlish who seemed happy to share. There was no ordering; the day's menus had been displayed in the Entrance Hall in the morning and they had all made their choices for the two main meals before eleven o'clock.

Some of the guests drank wine. The Colonel and Mr. Dawlish shared a bottle of Côtes du Rhone. A half-empty litre of Italian white wine with a stick-on label reading "Miss Vance" was on Eulalie's table when she arrived; from this she filled her glass regularly and took long, sighing draughts. Lady Ridgleigh had in front of her a bottle of Malvern water, though her conversation constantly implied that, but for her doctor's orders, she would be outdoing them all in her discriminating use of the wine list.

Mrs. Mendlingham and Miss Wardstone drank ordinary water. The latter did not hide her disapproval of alcoholic indulgence; many sniffs were heard whenever the subject was discussed. She frequently reasserted that she had never touched the beastly stuff and appeared to regard even the intake of food as a regrettably sybaritic necessity.

Mrs. Pargeter contented herself that night with a half-bottle of Beaujolais. It complemented Mrs. Denyer's excellent steak pie. The cabbage and carrots had also been carefully cooked, avoiding the curse of sogginess, which afflicts most English provincial cuisine.

Mrs. Pargeter was pleased. Her life with the late Mr. Pargeter had taught her to appreciate good food, and, after two dinners, she felt cautiously optimistic about the standards of the Devereux's kitchen.

The square dance quality of dinner at the Devereux also applied to the conversation, though here the rules were so complex that Mrs. Pargeter reckoned it might take her some time to understand them fully.

Colonel Wicksteed and Mr. Dawlish maintained their customary elliptical sequence of non sequiturs, but they were sitting at the same table. For the ladies, each marooned on her own island, the protocol was less straightforward. Remarks to the entire company were, of course, proscribed, but it was permissible for conversational lines to be cast from one island to the next. These castings were, however, erratic and discontinuous; no conversational flow could be said to have developed.

Mrs. Pargeter inwardly decided that something would have to be done to enliven this state of affairs. But, for that evening, she contented herself with almost complete silence.

What did strike her, though, was how little impact Mrs. Selsby's death had had. The old lady had slipped beneath the surface, causing scarcely a ripple to the still waters of life at the Devereux. Her image was already indistinct to Mrs. Pargeter, and seemed to be fading as fast for those residents who had known her longer. The Television Room was now unoccupied and none of the residents knew of its brief tenancy by a corpse.

As discreetly as the curtains close behind a coffin at a crematorium, a veil had been drawn over Mrs. Selsby's death.

Loxton was clearing the sweet plates (apple and blackberry crumble in Mrs. Pargeter's case, also excellent) and Newth busying himself with pouring coffee, when Miss Naismith swanned into the room. Basing her conclusion on two evenings at the Devereux, Mrs. Pargeter decided that this appearance must be a nightly occurrence.

It was a sort of "Everything all right?" call on behalf of the management (not of course so vulgar as a chef's appearance from the kitchen, nearer perhaps to a commanding officer's final tour of his encampment). It was an opportunity for any anxieties or complaints to be voiced by the residents.

Miss Naismith's entry also seemed to occupy the role with regard to television that the Loyal Toast does with regard to smoking. No one went into the Television Room before Miss Naismith appeared (though there might have been a little covert watching of portables in the bedrooms during the day).

But she did time her appearance tactfully at seven-twenty-five. This meant that on the relevant nights Colonel Wicksteed and Mr. Dawlish would not miss any of their favourite programme, *Coronation Street*. (This the two of them, neither of whom had ever in their lives travelled north of Cheltenham, watched with the fascinated bewilderment many people accord to Science Fiction.)

"Good evening," said Miss Naismith, using her privilege of addressing general remarks on the evening of the 5th of March. "I do hope that you have all had as pleasant a day as was possible . . . under the circumstances."

This was as near as her gentility would allow to a mention of Mrs. Selsby's death. But she need not have worried about offending any sensibilities; the mumbled chorus of affirmation suggested that none of them could think of any reason why they shouldn't have had a pleasant day.

Miss Naismith granted her new resident a glowing smile. "I trust you feel that you are settling in, Mrs. Pargeter."

"Yes, thank you, Miss Naismith," Mrs. Pargeter replied dutifully.

"Well, if there aren't any points anyone wishes to raise . . . ?" Miss Naismith inclined her body towards the door.

"There is something."

Miss Wardstone's voice came out too loud, with the harshness of someone who had never in her life attempted to make herself agreeable.

"Yes, Miss Wardstone?"

"When can I move in?"

"I beg your pardon?"

"Mrs. Selsby's room is now vacant. It has a sea-front position. It is the room that I quite clearly stated I wanted when I came to the Devereux. You said that I would be put on a waiting list for the room when it next became vacant. That moment has arrived, and I want to move in."

Miss Naismith's forehead wrinkled with pain at this lapse of etiquette. "Miss Wardstone, it is not yet twenty-four hours since Mrs. Selsby's . . . passing-on."

"I don't care. I want to get into that room. It's mine now."

"Yes, but—"

"I tried to get into the room this afternoon, but it was locked," said Miss Wardstone in a tone of accusation.

"Yes. Of course it is locked at the moment. I thought that was appropriate until Mrs. Selsby's relations or solicitor should arrive to take charge of her possessions."

"You can put them in a box-room or somewhere."

"No, Miss Wardstone. Mrs. Selsby had certain items of considerable value—jewellery in particular. I do have to think of the matter of security. It would be most inappropriate if anything were found to be missing when her possessions came to be claimed."

"Well, I want to get into that room." Miss Wardstone's reptilian jaw-line set hard and firm. "You said I would definitely be the next to go into it."

Miss Naismith refrigerated another smile. "I know that, Miss Wardstone. And I can assure you that I have no intention of going back on my word. The changeover will be made, but I do not think that it would be suitable to make it before Mrs. Selsby's funeral."

This was said with such finality that it reduced Miss Wardstone to only a sniff by way of riposte. Colonel Wicksteed and Mr. Dawlish took advantage of the change of mood to rise and, murmuring "We hope you will excuse us, ladies," to go off and watch what was left of *Coronation Street*.

Miss Naismith swept out after them.

Mrs. Pargeter looked at the expression of fury on Miss Wardstone's face. The spinster did want that sea-front room with an intensity that was almost obsessional.

But enough to kill for it? Of that Mrs. Pargeter was not yet sure.

11

Mrs. Pargeter rarely spoke of the late Mr. Pargeter, except in the most general terms. It was clear from her conversation that he had been a devoted husband, and also a wealthy one, who had left his widow exceptionally well-protected against the financial buffetings of the world. But, as Lady Ridgleigh had found out, enquiries into the sources of the late Mr. Pargeter's wealth were deflected by enigmatic answers.

Mrs. Pargeter, however, retained a deep and lasting affection for her late husband. Though his life had been unconventional, though their marriage had been interrupted by his occasional long absences, their love for each other had never faltered.

And Mrs. Pargeter had cause to be grateful to him for the many, many useful things that he had taught her.

She thought this once again as, at two-thirty in the morning of the 6th of March, she slipped the relevant blade of the late Mr. Pargeter's skeleton keys into the lock of the sea-front room that, until the previous day, had been occupied by Mrs. Selsby.

She was acting on intuition. Various ideas were connecting in her mind, but she needed more information to convert those connections into a solid chain of logic.

It was Mrs. Selsby's pearls that had put her on the track, and something Miss Naismith had said during the evening that had kept her going in the same direction. In Mrs. Selsby's room she hoped to find out whether she was proceeding on the high road to a solution or up a blind alley.

The lock gave and the door opened with the silent deference that characterised all the fittings of the Devereux. Inside the room the curtains were drawn, perhaps as a mark of respect to the deceased, but Mrs. Pargeter did not risk switching on the lights. Instead, she produced a small pencil torch, another invaluable legacy of the late Mr. Pargeter's working life.

She moved straight to the bureau in the bay window. In the front of the hotel she was much more aware of the insistent wash of the sea.

She wore gloves (another of the useful things the late Mr. Pargeter had taught her), and the well-oiled drawers of the bureau slid obligingly open at her touch. No need to use the skeleton keys again.

Mrs. Pargeter quickly found what she was looking for. Two drawers were full of slim black jewellery boxes. Screwing into her eye the jeweller's glass that the late Mr. Pargeter had also always found so useful, she expertly opened each box and examined its contents in the thin beam of her torch.

As she closed the last box, she smiled with satisfaction. She couldn't be sure about the settings, but every one of the precious stones confirmed her suspicions.

Mrs. Pargeter was silent as she left the sea-front room, and silent as she relocked the door with the skeleton key. She moved silently back up to her second-floor back bedroom, was quickly in bed, and quickly asleep.

Which was why she did not hear the sounds of someone else breaking into Mrs. Selsby's room later that night.

12

After breakfast on the morning of the 6th of March, Miss Naismith asked Mrs. Mendlingham whether she would mind stepping into the Office for a brief word. The expression in the old woman's wild eyes suggested that she would mind a lot, but she obediently followed the proprietress out of the Admiral's Dining Room.

"I wonder what that was about . . . ?"

Miss Wardstone voiced her conjecture to no one in particular. Apart from her, only Eulalie Vance and Mrs. Pargeter remained at their breakfast tables. Colonel Wicksteed had made his morning quip about time and tide, and soon been followed out by Mr. Dawlish and Lady Ridgleigh. Mrs. Pargeter sat relishing the last of her kipper, and Eulalie Vance stayed ostentatiously rereading a letter that had arrived by the morning post.

"I've no idea," said Mrs. Pargeter, politely picking up the conversational baton.

"A matter of personal hygiene, I wouldn't be surprised." Miss Wardstone sniffed vindictively, though whether this was an illustration of her words or the product of mere habit was not clear.

"Oh?" asked Mrs. Pargeter innocently.

"Come on. You must have smelled it. I'm afraid dear Mrs. Mendlingham is beginning rather to . . . lose control." Miss Wardstone emitted a little bark of unamused laughter and then added grimly, "I think she may be on the transfer list."

"Transfer list?"

"Miss Naismith is very insistent that the Devereux is for *active* people. In other words, people who are physically fit and in full control of themselves. I'm not sure that Mrs. Mendlingham any longer qualifies." Again a nasty little laugh.

"And where might she be transferred *to*?"

"The South Coast isn't short of Old People's Homes, Mrs. Pargeter. Private hotels like the Devereux are considerably rarer. And Miss Naismith is absolutely right to apply her rules with the maximum stringency."

Meaning, Mrs. Pargeter presumed, that Mrs. Mendlingham was being asked to find herself alternative accommodation. That could be a nasty shock for a person of her age, who might be driven to desperate courses to avoid such action taken against her.

Mrs. Pargeter wondered idly whether Mrs. Selsby had possessed any firm evidence of Mrs. Mendlingham's incontinence or other disqualifications from residency at the Devereux.

After her excursions of the day before, Mrs. Pargeter decided to stay in the hotel that morning. In her enquiries into Mrs. Selsby's death, she still felt that listening was going to be the most productive approach.

Her first encounter did not prove very illuminating. Having finished her kipper and indulged in one final cup of tea, Mrs. Pargeter took her *Daily Mail* into the Seaview Lounge, where she found Lady Ridgleigh wincing over half-glasses at her copy of *The Times*. The same string of pearls, she noticed, hung around the thin neck, this time vying with a red and blue check patterned dress. After her expedition during the night, Mrs. Pargeter found that she was thinking a lot about jewellery. Lady Ridgleigh's pearls, her expert eye reaffirmed, were exquisite and very valuable.

The Times was ceremoniously folded and laid flat across bony knees. The half-glasses were placed in a monogrammed case. Lady Ridgleigh, it was clear, was about to make a conversational effort.

Assuming the expression of interest that the Queen adopts when asking Commonwealth leaders about new hydro-electric installations, she said, "Well, I do hope you'll be very happy here, Mrs. Pargeter."

"I'm sure I will. I had a look round the town yesterday. Littlehampton seems a very nice little place."

Lady Ridgleigh did not appear completely convinced of the truth of the assertion. "Some of it is very pleasant, certainly. Not as select, perhaps, as Rustington or Middleton-on-Sea. Or, of course, dear Bognor. Still, some of it is quite adequate. Other parts, I fear, are rather less salubrious."

"Oh?"

"I am afraid so. The summer can be very distressing."

"Oh dear."

"Bank Holidays are particularly unpleasant. I make a point of not stirring outside the hotel's doors on Bank Holidays."

"Why?"

"The tone is lowered considerably. There have even been instances of violence on the front."

"From whom?"

Lady Ridgleigh's bony shoulders shuddered. "I believe they call themselves 'Hell's Angels.' "

"Oh dear."

"Yes." Lady Ridgleigh straightened her back. "It makes me so thankful that we have the Royal Family."

Mrs. Pargeter could think of no appropriate rejoinder for this, and so started to read her *Daily Mail*. Lady Ridgleigh, feeling that she had displayed quite sufficient "common touch" for one day, put her half-glasses back on, reopened her *Times* and found the "Court and Social" page.

The next arrival in the Seaview Lounge was Colonel Wicksteed, returning rather earlier than usual from his "constitutional." He rubbed his hands together as he came in.

"Couldn't stay out long this morning. Damned cold." He stopped short. "Pardon my French, ladies."

Lady Ridgleigh's bony hand waved gracious forgiveness, and the Colonel deposited himself in his customary armchair in the bay window. The binoculars, around his neck when he entered, were at once raised to scan the slaty expanse of the sea.

In a matter of moments, Mr. Dawlish, somehow sensing his friend's return, entered and, with little bows to the ladies, took his seat opposite the Colonel. He arranged the rug about his thin knees.

"Anything?"

"No." The Colonel lowered his binoculars to his lap. "Not a thing." He sighed. "No." Then a furtive expression crept across his face as, after looking round elaborately, he said in a hoarse whisper, "Saw something this morning rather tickled me."

"Oh?"

Mr. Dawlish adopted an equally exaggerated whisper. The effect of both was to draw attention to what they were saying rather than to obscure it, but, with an amateur dramatic society prompter's confidence in his inaudibility, the Colonel continued.

"Saw it in the newsagent—went in there to buy the *Sporting*—erm, erm . . . *Horse and Hound* and—"

"Where is it?"

"What?"

"*Horse and Hound.*"

"Oh, erm, they hadn't got it. Anyway in the newsagent, I happened to glance at some of those, er . . . you know, those things they have in there . . . bit near the knuckle. . . ."

"Gloves?" Mr. Dawlish offered helpfully.

"No, no. Postcards," the Colonel hissed.

"Oh yes. Postcards."

"Know the sort I mean?"

"Of course." Mr. Dawlish nodded contentedly. " 'View of West Beach,' 'View of the Arun Estuary,' 'View of—' "

"No, no, not those." The Colonel leant forward and became even more elaborately conspiratorial. "I mean postcards with a bit of spice."

"I've never come across those," said Mr. Dawlish. "Whatever will they think of next?"

The Colonel shook his head impatiently, but decided to press on with his story. "Anyway, one of these postcards had this picture of a . . . young woman . . . know what I mean?"

Mr. Dawlish nodded.

"And she was extremely . . . what's the word?"

"I've no idea," replied Mr. Dawlish with disarming honesty.

"Well endowed . . . know what I mean?"

"Oh yes." Mr. Dawlish nodded. "Got lots of money for her old age."

"No, no. When I say 'well endowed,' I mean 'well endowed' . . ." The Colonel dropped his voice even lower ". . . *physically*. Anyway, there she is, scantily clad, looking quite pleased with herself, sitting on the side of a bed—husband in bed asleep—and she's writing a letter. . . . Bet you can't guess what the caption is . . . ?"

No, Mr. Dawlish couldn't guess what the caption was.

" 'Dear Sirs,' " Colonel Wicksteed hissed. " 'Last night I used some of your ointment on my husband's recommendation and there's been a great improvement.' " He stifled a guffaw. "Do you get it?"

"No," Mr. Dawlish replied evenly.

The Colonel shook his head and sank back despairingly into his chair. "No," he echoed.

There was a long silence in the bay window.

Then Mr. Dawlish volunteered that he had once used some ointment on his doctor's recommendation.

"Ah," said Colonel Wicksteed.

"But there was no improvement."

"Ah. Well . . ."

"No. Never cleared up. Still got the ruddy thing."

"Oh."

They lapsed again into silence. Mrs. Pargeter, deciding that her investigation was not progressing much in the Seaview Lounge, rose and, with polite smiles of farewell, left the room.

13

In the hall she met Miss Naismith, who had on her face an expression compounded of surprise, distaste and sheer triumph.

"Ah, Mrs. Pargeter," she said with a smile that made no attempt at geniality. "I was just coming to look for you. I wonder if you would be so kind as to step into my Office for a brief word."

Mrs. Pargeter saw no objection to doing this. Inside the Office was a balding man wearing a pin-striped suit and a look of professional disapproval.

"Mrs. Pargeter—this is Mr. Holland. He is the late Mrs. Selsby's solicitor, who has come down to take charge of her affairs."

"How do you do?" Mrs. Pargeter offered a plump hand, which was shaken without enthusiasm.

"Shall we all sit down?" suggested Miss Naismith.

They sat, and she looked at Mr. Holland to begin the proceedings.

"The fact is, Mrs. Pargeter, that, as Miss Naismith said, I have, since the death of her husband—incidentally, her last surviving relative—handled Mrs. Selsby's affairs. As soon as I could after hearing the sad news of her . . . er, passing-on . . ." (Mrs. Pargeter had the feeling that this was not the expression he would instinctively have used. Maybe Miss Naismith had already rapped him over the knuckles that morning for insufficient delicacy.) ". . . I came down here to make suitable arrangements. Now I believe that you have only recently moved into the hotel . . ."

"That's right."

". . . but perhaps you are aware that Mrs. Selsby was the owner of a considerable amount of jewellery."

"I had heard that, yes."

"Now, unwisely, and against my advice, Mrs. Selsby was in the habit of leaving this valuable jewellery around her hotel room."

"Against my advice, too," Miss Naismith righteously interposed. "I constantly recommended her to put such valuables in the hotel safe. As Lady Ridgleigh does with her extensive collection of jewellery. But Mrs. Selsby wouldn't hear of it. 'No,' she would repeatedly say. 'I like to have it near me, where I can look at it.' "

"Which was rather ironic, wasn't it," said Mrs. Pargeter, "considering that her eyesight was so bad?"

"Be that as it may. . . ." Mr. Holland's tone implied that he did not like having his monologue interrupted. "Needless to say, one of my first actions on arriving here was to check the inventory of jewellery that I knew Mrs. Selsby to possess."

"Of course." Mrs. Pargeter smiled.

72

"Now, I asked Miss Naismith where Mrs. Selsby kept her jewellery and discovered that it was her rather careless custom to leave it in unlocked drawers of her bureau."

Mrs. Pargeter nodded. She felt confident she knew what was coming.

But she was wrong. The words that did come took her breath away as if they had been physical blows.

"Imagine my surprise then, Mrs. Pargeter, when I found all of Mrs. Selsby's bureau drawers to be empty."

Mrs. Pargeter gaped.

"Needless to say, I immediately searched the rest of the room, but found nothing. Which leads me to the unpleasant conclusion that Mrs. Selsby's jewellery has been stolen."

"Which is a very regrettable word for me to hear used in this establishment," said Miss Naismith. "There have never been any thefts here before, and an uncharitable enquiry into the incident might first ask the question . . . who is the most recent arrival in the hotel?"

"If you are suggesting I stole the jewellery, Miss Naismith, I'd advise you to be careful. It's not the sort of accusation that should be thrown around lightly."

Miss Naismith was enjoying herself. "I agree. Nor would I throw it around lightly. However, when I have a witness to the fact that one of the hotel residents broke into Mrs. Selsby's locked room at half-past two last night, I feel the circumstances may be a little different."

Mrs. Pargeter did not allow herself to be rattled. "What are you saying?"

Mr. Holland took over the indelicate situation. "Miss Naismith is saying that *you* were seen breaking into the room last night. Since she checked that the jewels were in place before locking the room yesterday morning, there can be little doubt that you stole them. Which is why, I am afraid, we will be obliged to telephone for the police."

Mrs. Pargeter still did not reveal any emotion. Nor did she make any attempt to deny her actions. "May I ask you who saw me enter Mrs. Selsby's room?"

"Mrs. Mendlingham. She was on the landing."

Miss Naismith no longer attempted to hide her triumph. On first meeting Mrs. Pargeter, she had recognised that conflict between them was inevitable. But she had expected that the conflict would be a long-drawn-out campaign of attrition. To have her adversary play so quickly and clumsily into her hands was more than the proprietress of the Devereux had dared hope for.

14

Mrs. Pargeter folded her plump hands on her lap.

"So . . . you are going to call the police?"

"Yes." On the face of someone less genteel, Miss Naismith's expression would have been described as a leer. "Can you tell me any reason why we shouldn't?"

"No. None at all. I'm sure, in the event of a robbery in a hotel like this, the police should definitely be informed."

"Good. I'm glad you agree." Miss Naismith nodded to Mr. Holland, who reached towards the telephone on her desk.

"On the other hand," Mrs. Pargeter continued without raising her voice, "I think you would be very ill-advised to make the same accusation to the police as you have to me."

Mr. Holland's hand stopped in mid-air.

"Oh. And why do you think that?" asked Miss Naismith, as usual accentuating the "h" in "why."

"I think it because I did not take the jewels. I don't deny going into Mrs. Selsby's room last night. I don't deny taking the jewels out of the bureau and looking at them. But I then put them back."

"Well, of course you'd *say* that."

"Anyway, *why* should you behave in the bizarre manner you describe?" asked Mr. Holland, modelling himself on some severe barrister from a television court-room drama.

"That, for the moment, is my business."

"If you aren't prepared to explain yourself, Miss Naismith and I can hardly be blamed for placing the construction that we have on your actions. I'm afraid I do feel obliged to call the police."

Once again his hand reached for the telephone, but once again it was frozen by Mrs. Pargeter's soft voice.

"I think you need rather more evidence for your accusation. If I did take the jewels, where do you think they are now?"

"Well, I hadn't really considered . . ."

"No. According to your theory, I stole the jewels at two-thirty this morning. Now the security in this hotel is good. The burglar alarm system works with pressure pads by the doors and windows of the front of the building and contact breakers on the doors at the back."

"How do you know that?" asked Miss Naismith, surprised.

"I make a habit of being observant," Mrs. Pargeter replied evenly. She did not say that the habit of observing security systems was another of the useful things she had learnt from the late Mr. Pargeter.

"I'm not quite clear where this is getting us," said Mr. Holland in a tone of professional impatience.

"What I am saying is that it would have been impossible for me to get out of the hotel quietly until after Newth had switched off the burglar alarm this morning. And since that time, as any of the residents can confirm, I have not left the premises."

"So?"

Mrs. Pargeter sighed with exasperation. The solicitor really was being very obtuse. "So, since I haven't left the premises, if I stole the jewels, they can't have left the premises either."

"Well . . ."

"Unless, of course, I had an accomplice . . . Yes, perhaps I took Newth into my confidence. He after all has the keys to the alarm system—not to mention a pass key to Mrs. Selsby's room."

Miss Naismith coloured. "How dare you, Mrs. Pargeter? I will not have such imputations made about one of my staff."

"You seemed quite happy to make such imputations about one of your guests," Mrs. Pargeter observed mildly.

"So what you are saying . . . ?"asked Mr. Holland.

Really he wasn't very intelligent. Still, Mrs. Pargeter reflected, you didn't have to be very intelligent to be a solicitor. Just somehow scrape through a few exams in your twenties and then the British legal system saw to it that you had a meal ticket for life.

"What I am saying," she explained patiently, "is that, if you really believe I stole the jewels, all you have to do is to search my room, or—crediting me with a little subtlety—search the rest of the hotel, and you will find evidence to convict me, won't you?"

"Ye-es." Mr. Holland sounded uncertain.

"Such a search," said Miss Naismith with distaste, "would be very upsetting to the other residents."

At this Mrs. Pargeter finally lost her temper. Without forfeiting her considerable dignity, she snapped, "Listen, if you're prepared to upset me so easily, I don't give a damn about your upsetting the other residents! You have to face the fact, Miss Naismith, that, repellent though it may be to your sensibilities, a robbery has taken place in the Devereux. And the circumstances of that robbery mean it was committed either by one of the residents or by one of the staff. Now it would be extremely convenient if I had committed it, because you could then quietly ask me to leave, and sweep the whole matter under the carpet.

"Unfortunately for you, I didn't do it, so you are faced with the unpleasant prospect of starting an enquiry into the activities of the other people who live in this hotel."

"Ah, you *say* you didn't do it. . . ."

"Yes, and, as I mentioned before, a search of the premises will *prove* I didn't do it. And, if you once again make the accusation that I *did* do it, let me assure you I will get in touch with my solicitor and see to it that you pay me very substantial damages."

At last Mr. Holland felt they were on to a subject he knew something about. "Might I ask," he enquired superciliously, "who your solicitor is?"

"I deal with the Justiman Partnership."

"Oh." He was impressed. "Might I ask who in particular you deal with there?"

"I have always had my affairs handled by Arnold Justiman."

This was another of her fortunate legacies from the

late Mr. Pargeter. Her husband had been a constant employer of Arnold Justiman, one of the most eminent of his profession, and Mrs. Pargeter often reflected that she owed much of her conjugal happiness to Arnold Justiman. Without his good offices, Mr. Pargeter's occasional necessary absences from the marital home would have been much longer.

"Oh. Arnold Justiman himself." Mr. Holland was now *very* impressed. He sat back in his chair with hands folded on his lap, as if to dismiss any idea that they might ever have contemplated reaching for a telephone. "I think, Miss Naismith, we would be very ill-advised to pursue this line of enquiry."

"What?" asked Mrs. Pargeter with a hint of mockery. "You don't want to find out who stole the jewels?"

"Well, yes, we do. Of course we do. And in the fullness of time, in consultation with the proper authorities, I am sure that we will. I was merely suggesting that we should not be too precipitate in our actions. Wouldn't you agree, Miss Naismith?"

"Yes, yes, I would."

The proprietress looked as if she had just swallowed something singularly disgusting and was faced with more unpalatable mouthfuls ahead. Mrs. Pargeter's openness and ready suggestion of a search had convinced her accuser that the blame for the theft lay elsewhere. That raised the unpleasant prospect of investigating the other residents of the Devereux.

And also Miss Naismith had the uncomfortable knowledge that she had overplayed her hand and allowed her antipathy to Mrs. Pargeter to become too nakedly apparent.

"Well, don't let me keep you any longer." Mrs. Pargeter rose from her chair. "On the strict understanding that the matter is never raised again, I am quite happy to forget what has been said here this morning." She smiled sweetly at her accusers. "And do let me know if there is anything I can do to help you in your investigations into this unfortunate incident."

She moved to the door, but stopped before she opened it.

"Oh, one thing, Miss Naismith . . . I wonder, would it be possible for me to hand my jewellery to you to be kept in the hotel safe . . . ? It would be most regrettable if there were another lapse of security at the Devereux, wouldn't it?"

"Yes. Yes, of course that would be possible," Miss Naismith replied, tight-lipped.

"Might I have a look at the safe?" asked Mrs. Pargeter charmingly. "Unless it's of a reputable manufacture, I might decide I'd be better advised to put my valuables in the bank."

Wordlessly, Miss Naismith moved an embroidered fire-screen to reveal a square grey metal box, on which a silver plate bore the legend, "Clissold & Fry—Excalibur Two."

"Oh, yes, that will be quite adequate. If I may, I'll bring my jewellery down as soon as possible. If that's convenient . . . ?"

"Of course. Any time," said Miss Naismith with a ghastly smile, as Mrs. Pargeter moved gracefully out of the Office.

15

In the Entrance Hall Mrs. Pargeter paused for a moment of grim satisfaction. She had no doubt that she had seen off Miss Naismith, but she was still angry that the accusation had ever been made. None of the other residents would have been attacked frontally in that manner, and, though usually Mrs. Pargeter was the most tolerant of individuals, another legacy of her life with the late Mr. Pargeter was a certain sensitivity to imputations of criminal behaviour.

Still, she thought with a wicked little surge of glee, she had effectively diverted them from questions about what she *was* doing in Mrs. Selsby's room in the middle of the night.

She looked out through the glass of the closed front doors to the greyness beyond, and saw a small figure wound up in a plum-coloured coat walking briskly away from the hotel on the other side of the road. In spite of the black fur hat pulled down over the ears, she had no difficulty in recognising Mrs. Mendlingham.

Mrs. Pargeter decided she might put her own coat on and go for a walk.

The coat in question was a mink, which the late Mr. Pargeter, always the soul of generosity, had presented to her after a particularly successful business venture, and that morning she was glad of its warmth. The weather, which had not been good for some time, seemed now to have lapsed into icy melancholy, as if it had lost faith in the idea of there ever being a summer. The wind carried a stinging spray—or maybe it was rain—and the sea was lost about fifty yards out in sticky fog.

It was not a morning for recreational walking, and Mrs. Pargeter wondered where Mrs. Mendlingham was headed with such apparent determination. As she emerged from the Devereux and felt the first breath-snatching blast of the weather, Mrs. Pargeter could still see the small plum-coloured figure striding along the front and, without hurrying, she had no difficulty in keeping her quarry in sight.

Mrs. Mendlingham was walking along towards the Arun estuary, past the closed Smart's Amusements, on whose wall even the perky figure of Mickey Mouse looked forlorn. The exposed metalwork of the mini-roller-coaster known as the Mouse Run gave the edifice the unfinished look of a building site. Mrs. Mendlingham continued straight ahead, past the sad fairy-tale turrets of the Giant Slide.

Mrs. Pargeter was intrigued. Her reconnaissance of Littlehampton two days before had been thorough and, as far as she could remember, Mrs. Mendlingham appeared to be walking into a dead end, a little corner between the beach and the river.

Suddenly the plum-coloured figure was no longer visible.

Mrs. Pargeter did not increase her pace. There was nowhere Mrs. Mendlingham could have gone, except into one of the sea-front shelters.

These concrete structures were designed to keep the wind off the bench seats inside them, and on days when the wind was less blustery and erratic, perhaps they did. That morning they seemed only to attract little eddies of cold air, providing a home for the small hurricanes of the sea front. In one or two of them Mrs. Pargeter saw old people propped in the corners, faces purple with cold between their scarves and hats, but showing rigid determination to get away for a little while from the four walls of their homes (or their Homes).

Mrs. Mendlingham was not sitting in the first group of shelters, but there were some others farther on, with glass partitions, which faced over the river rather than the sea. As she rounded the corner of one of these, Mrs. Pargeter saw the plum-coloured figure she was seeking. Mrs. Mendlingham was hunched against the end wall of the shelter. One hand in a fingerless woolen glove held a hard-covered black notebook, while the other wrote in it at great speed.

"Good morning."

The old wild eyes darted up sharply at Mrs. Pargeter's words, and in one movement, almost too quick to be seen, the notebook and pen were concealed under the folds of the plum-coloured coat.

"Good morning," said Mrs. Mendlingham. There was a slyness in her voice, the tone of someone congratulating herself on a successful deception.

"Do you mind if I join you?"

Mrs. Mendlingham's expression was not welcoming, but she voiced no objection as Mrs. Pargeter sat on the bench and swaddled herself in the mink coat.

In front of them the Arun flowed murkily. The tide was going out. A small fishing dinghy with an outboard motor swept past, tide-assisted, as if it were a power boat. The cold wind swirled and eddied around them.

"You come out here to write?" asked Mrs. Pargeter.

Again the old face filled with suspicion and cunning. "What if I do?"

"Difficult to get privacy at the Devereux, I find. Even after my brief stay."

"What do you mean?"

"It's the sort of place where everything you do seems to be observed."

This didn't prompt any reaction, so Mrs. Pargeter made her point even clearer. "Last night I was seen going into Mrs. Selsby's room."

There was a sly smile from Mrs. Mendlingham. "Yes."

"An unlikely time to be awake . . ."

"I don't sleep well these days."

"No. No, it does seem more difficult as one gets older, doesn't it? Do you have anything to help you sleep?"

Mrs. Mendlingham snorted dismissively. "The doctor gives me pills. They work for a little while. But after two or three hours I wake again."

Mrs. Pargeter nodded. "Every night?"

"Most nights."

"How did you come to see me last night? I didn't see you."

"I heard footsteps and just opened my door a little."

"Yes, of course, you're on the first floor, aren't you?"

Mrs. Pargeter paused before continuing, gently, "And I suppose you'd do that any night. . . . If you happened to be awake, and hear footsteps, you'd open your door a little to see who it was . . . ?"

"I expect I would, yes," replied Mrs. Mendlingham, unguarded.

Mrs. Pargeter suddenly made her enquiry less languid. "Two nights ago, the night Mrs. Selsby died, I heard a commotion and a little cry on the first-floor landing. What did you see that night?"

The old lady looked shocked. She opened and closed her mouth a few times before replying. "I saw nothing that night. I didn't hear anything. I slept through that night."

"Ah," Mrs. Pargeter murmured peaceably. "Rather a pity, that, wasn't it?"

"Why?"

"Well, if you'd heard something, you might have been able to save Mrs. Selsby."

"I hardly think so. She died immediately." Fearing that this had given away too much, Mrs. Mendlingham lamely added, "I gather."

"Yes. Yes. That's what I gather, too," Mrs. Pargeter reassured her. "Did you know Mrs. Selsby well?" she asked diffidently.

"No. No. Well, you get to know people when you're living in the same building, of course you do. But I didn't know her well, no."

"Did you like her?"

The shoulders shrugged in the plum-coloured coat. "We were hardly soul-mates. She was a bit of a busybody."

"Always nosing her way into other people's business, you mean?"

"Yes."

"A bit of a tell-tale, too . . . ?" Mrs. Pargeter floated this idea with care. She had no basis but instinct for the suggestion. "Tended to sneak to Miss Naismith, did she . . . ?"

Her instinct had been right.

"Yes," Mrs. Mendlingham replied. "Always. If she found out a secret about someone, she was incapable of keeping it to herself."

"Did she find out anything about you . . . ?"

Mrs. Mendlingham opened her mouth to reply, then thought better of it and took refuge in her old-lady vagueness. "I don't know what you're talking about."

Not for the first time, Mrs. Pargeter found herself wondering how much of an act Mrs. Mendlingham's senility was. Frequently the old lady appeared almost completely gaga, but she was also capable of sustained concentration, and at times the sharp intelligence in her faded eyes was positively disturbing.

Mrs. Pargeter tried another tack. "Miss Naismith asked to see you this morning."

The old eyes stared unfocused towards the dunes on the other side of the river. Mrs. Pargeter repeated her sentence.

"What? Oh yes." But Mrs. Mendlingham still seemed to be giving only part of her attention.

"Apart from your telling her about seeing me last night, may I ask what else you talked about?"

Mrs. Mendlingham was too disturbed by the thought of Miss Naismith to notice the directness of Mrs. Pargeter's inquisition. "Miss Naismith," she mumbled, "is a cruel woman."

"Cruel because she wants you to move out of the Devereux?" hazarded Mrs. Pargeter.

This was greeted by a little cracked laugh. "She won't succeed, you know. You can get anything you want in

86

this life with money. That's all she cares about. For all her airs, Miss Naismith will do anything for the right amount of money."

In the strange atmosphere between them Mrs. Pargeter felt she could risk another impertinent question. "Are you a wealthy woman, Mrs. Mendlingham?"

She got no reply except another laugh, but it was a laugh full of confidence, cunning and even triumph, a laugh that said, "Yes, now I'm a very wealthy woman."

"And you're still sure you saw nothing on the first-floor landing two nights ago?"

The eyes came into sudden sharp focus. "Nothing." The word was almost spat out. "Nothing. Nothing happened on the landing that night. You'll never find out about anything happening on the landing that night. And I wouldn't advise you to be nosey, Mrs. . . . Mrs. Whatever-your-name-is. Nosey people can get hurt, you know."

Abruptly, with another manic giggle, Mrs. Mendlingham rose to her feet, shook her coat around her, pulled her fur hat down over her ears, and set off walking briskly along the front towards the Devereux.

16

Mrs. Pargeter did not follow. She did not think that she would elicit much more from Mrs. Mendlingham that morning. Besides, the information she had got was plenty to set her thinking, to start all kinds of hares racing across her mind. So she sat, pensively cocooned in her mink, until her feet began to grow numb with cold. Then she rose and briskly followed Mrs. Mendlingham's route back to the Devereux.

When she had taken off her coat and boots, she went down to the Seaview Lounge. It was about half an hour till lunchtime, and the room was empty, except for the solicitor, Mr. Holland.

He rose a little awkwardly as she entered, and when she was settled into an armchair, said, "I must apologise for this morning."

Mrs. Pargeter smiled equably. "Think nothing of it."

"I'm afraid, not knowing the residents of the hotel as individuals, I was perhaps too easily swayed by Miss Naismith's views as to what might have happened to Mrs. Selsby's jewels."

"Of course. Perfectly understandable. By the way, has Miss Naismith organised a search of the hotel?"

"Tentative steps have been taken. She accompanied the chambermaid . . . is her name Loxton? . . . on her morning bed-making round and examined the obvious hiding places."

"A waste of time looking in the obvious places. Whoever took those jewels would have hidden them very thoroughly. Hmm. I wonder if Miss Naismith has investigated the hotel's rubbish . . . ?"

"Rubbish? But surely no one would risk putting valuable jewels in with the rubbish?"

"I don't think you know a lot about the criminal mind, Mr. Holland."

"I am a solicitor," he said, affronted.

"Yes, but you have to get *inside* the criminal mind to find out what they're likely to do. Anyway, in this case . . ." But Mrs. Pargeter decided she was perhaps giving away too much about herself and stopped short. "Presumably, nothing was found—none of the boxes, nothing?"

Mr. Holland shook his head ruefully.

"Oh well, the police will no doubt be more thorough."

"Er, yes . . ."

The note of hesitation in his voice made Mrs. Pargeter look up sharply. "Do you mean she hasn't called the police yet?"

"I'm afraid not. Against my advice, I may say. Miss Naismith felt it might be more discreet if she were to wait for twenty-four hours and see if the jewels should reappear."

"Why on earth should they suddenly reappear? What does she think they've done—gone on a day trip to Boulogne?"

"No, no. Miss Naismith's view is that, if she lets it be known amongst the residents that certain articles have been noted as missing from Mrs. Selsby's room, someone's memory might be jogged and the jewels might indeed suddenly . . . er, reappear," he finished lamely.

"I see." A light of anger burned in Mrs. Pargeter's eye. "She was quite happy to have *me* drummed out of the place, but if anyone else is the culprit, she'll just gloss it over."

Mr. Holland looked intensely uncomfortable. "As I say, Miss Naismith is acting against my advice."

Mrs. Pargeter nodded grimly. "Oh yes. Hmm. I wonder if perhaps I should get in touch with Arnold Justiman after all. . . ."

The name once again had its predictable effect on Mr. Holland. Considerably flustered, he assured Mrs. Pargeter that such a course of action would not be at all necessary. "As I say, Miss Naismith has just twenty-four hours to conduct her internal enquiry. If that reveals nothing, then there is no question of the police not being brought in."

"Hmm," Mrs. Pargeter decided to take advantage of the solicitor's abjectly apologetic state to pump him for information. "Were Mrs. Selsby's jewels worth a lot?"

"A very considerable amount," he replied smugly.

"How much?" Mrs. Pargeter had long since learned the surprise value of direct questioning.

"Oh, erm, well . . ." Mr. Holland succumbed. "At their last valuation for insurance—which was two years ago—the total sum was eleven and a half thousand pounds."

Mrs. Pargeter nodded, pleased to have had her own estimate confirmed. "And, presumably, the jewels were not the full extent of her possessions?"

The solicitor almost chuckled at the naïveté of the idea. "Oh, my goodness me, no. Mrs. Selsby was a very wealthy woman."

"And with no living relatives . . ."

Mr. Holland did not volunteer the information she had hoped for, so Mrs. Pargeter resorted to another direct question. "Who inherits?"

The solicitor blushed at the unprofessional nature of this enquiry. "I don't think it is yet appropriate for me to divulge details of, er—"

"Never mind," said Mrs. Pargeter. "I'll get on to Arnold. His information-gathering service is remarkable. I'm sure he could find out for me very quickly."

"Oh, er, well, in that case . . ." Mr. Holland wavered. "I suppose the details are to be public soon enough. . . . I doubt if much harm could be done by . . . And since you aren't a beneficiary . . ."

Mrs. Pargeter laughed. "Of course I'm not. I only met her once. Why should I be a beneficiary?"

"That, Mrs. Pargeter, is one of the strange features of the will. Mrs. Selsby, as you just said, had no living relatives, no one in fact very close to her—except for the people living in this hotel."

"Oh?"

"She was happy here. She found the Devereux a dignified and genteel place in which to spend the, er, evening of her life. And so, two years ago, she summoned me and asked me to draw up a will, which divided her estate equally between all of the people living in the Devereux."

"Staff as well?"

"Yes. Miss Naismith and Newth were to be included. Loxton, too, although she does not actually live on the premises. Mrs. Selsby's only stipulation was that the beneficiaries should have been here for at least six months. Which is why," he explained, apologetically, "as I said, I'm afraid you fail to qualify."

The late Mr. Pargeter had left his widow sufficiently well cushioned to accept this news with equanimity. "But that's a very unusual will, isn't it?"

"Yes," Mr. Holland replied with some asperity. "And a very ill-advised one. I spelled out to Mrs. Selsby all of the arguments against such a course, its potential dangers and disadvantages, but she was adamant. That was how she wanted it to be."

Mrs. Pargeter was struck that Mr. Holland must be a very weak man. He was employed as a professional adviser and yet no one seemed to take his advice. Mrs. Selsby had ignored him, and he had allowed Miss Naismith to ride roughshod over him that morning. Weak and stupid, she decided.

"So . . ." she said slowly, "everyone in the Devereux stood to benefit from Mrs. Selsby's death. . . ."

"Well, I think that's a rather cynical way of putting it, but, under the terms of her will, everyone would inherit an equal share, yes."

"How much money are we talking about?" Mr. Holland winced at the indelicacy of this question. "Come on. How much? Five thousand? Ten thousand? Twenty thousand? Fifty thousand? A hundred thousand?"

Pained at the necessity of replying, he said quietly, "Nearer your final figure than the others."

Mrs. Pargeter nodded. "And do you know if any of

the people living here were aware of the unusual provisions of this will?"

"Of that I have no idea." And, feeling perhaps that he had let down his professional image, Mr. Holland added huffily, "But I can't see that it's important."

No, thought Mrs. Pargeter, you wouldn't be able to see that, would you?

But it is important. Very.

17

6 MARCH—10:45 p.m.—*It is strange—or perhaps even amusing—to see how quickly my thoughts are once again turning to murder. After my first, eminently successful, foray, which so simply—and even elegantly—achieved what I needed, one might have expected a period of peace and recuperation, a period of resting on my laurels, before thoughts of murder should once again begin to dominate my mind.*

But that, I fear, is not to be. Already I am experiencing that cliché of history and literature—the fact that one crime very easily leads to another. I can understand how this unalterable rule of human life might cause considerable anguish to those afflicted with a conscience, to those who commit one murder on the premise that it is a once-and-for-all solution to an intolerable problem, and then find themselves drawn inexorably on to new murders.

For me, of course, such considerations do not matter. Since removing Mrs. Selsby, I have still felt no pang of remorse—indeed, no emotion at all, except for a certain smug satisfaction.

My new target is another lady—one, who, I fear, is already showing far too much interest in Mrs. Selsby's death. I do not yet know how much she knows, but I fear the worst. What she does not actually know, she may deduce, and that is a risk that I do not at the moment wish to take. Though reconciled to the possibility that my new career may end in my apprehension by the police, I do not wish to invite such an outcome. I think I will enjoy the short time left to me better if I retain my freedom.

Besides, imprisonment would rather limit my opportunities for committing other murders. For, yes, here in my diary I can make the confession that would be inadmissible anywhere else: I derived immense satisfaction from my first murder, and, though I pretend to myself that committing the second will be an unfortunate necessity, it is in fact something that I look forward to with enormous excitement.

18

On the morning of the 7th of March the inquest on Mrs. Selsby was held in Worthing.

Newth was present as the one who had discovered the body; Dr. Ashington was present as Mrs. Selsby's physician and as the one who had examined the body; Mr. Holland was there as a representative of the deceased; and Miss Naismith was there, because she was the proprietress of the Devereux and felt that she should know about everything that concerned the hotel.

As Dr. Ashington had predicted, there were no complications. Mrs. Selsby, because of her considerable frailty and failing eyesight, was reckoned to have taken a false step on the landing of the Devereux Hotel and fallen down the stairs. No negligence was attributable to anyone, and a verdict of Accidental Death was recorded.

When the inquest party had returned to the Devereux, another formal meeting was held. All of the residents, along with Newth and Loxton, were summoned to the Seaview Lounge by Miss Naismith and told that Mr. Holland had an announcement to make.

Although Mrs. Pargeter had a shrewd idea that the announcement did not concern her, she went to the Lounge and made a point of sitting in a chair against the wall opposite the bay window, from which position she could see the faces of all of the others.

As soon as they were assembled (they had to wait ten minutes for Mrs. Mendlingham, who had apparently dozed off in her room), Mr. Holland turned to Mrs. Pargeter and confirmed what she had anticipated.

"I regret, Mrs. Pargeter, that, for reasons of which I believe you are aware, what I have to say does not apply to you. If you would rather leave us to discuss the matter on our own . . . ?"

"No, no. I'm fine here," she replied breezily.

Mr. Holland, perhaps, recognising that he could not bring any spark of intelligence or originality to his work, made sure that he brought a full measure of pomposity. Addressing a large assembly gave him ample opportunity to show off his armoury of long words and convoluted syntax, and he indulged this to such an extent that there was a long and confusing preamble before he got to the meat of his message.

While he rambled on, Mrs. Pargeter covertly glanced around, noting the expressions of the listeners. Miss Naismith looked serenely genteel, displaying, as was proper, no emotion; and yet Mrs. Pargeter felt certain that the proprietress knew the burden of the solicitor's message. Colonel Wicksteed looked acutely interested, as if he were watching a cricket match; Mr. Dawlish vaguely confused, as if he were trying to find out where the cricket match was being played.

Miss Wardstone bore an expression of reptilian smugness, and Eulalie Vance looked as if she were selecting which of her vast wardrobe of reactions should be shown off when Mr. Holland's dénouement came. Lady Ridgleigh's eyes were closed, and the bony fingers of one hand were pressed to her temple, as if she had a headache. Newth and Loxton looked respectful, if slightly bored, and on Mrs. Mendlingham's face was a look of pure, evil glee.

It would be interesting, Mrs. Pargeter thought, to see how those expressions changed when the announcement was finally made.

". . . and the provisions of this extremely unusual will are that the residue of her estate shall be divided equally amongst those residents and full-time staff of the Devereux Hotel who have been here for more than six months." He turned to Mrs. Pargeter. "Which is why, of course, I began by apologising to you."

But she did not hear his words. She was far too interested in the changing faces of the others in the room.

Miss Naismith, as anticipated, showed no reaction, save possibly a more serene serenity.

Colonel Wicksteed kept slapping his thigh and saying, "Well, I'll be damned!"

Mr. Dawlish let out a thin, high, continuous giggle.

Miss Wardstone's smugness deepened, while Eulalie Vance kept clapping her hands together and emitting inappropriately girlish cries of joy.

Lady Ridgleigh had slumped back in her chair with an

abandonment that might have arisen from exhaustion or from relief.

Newth looked pale and was pressing a hand to his chest. Loxton had suddenly and unaccountably burst into tears.

And Mrs. Mendlingham's glee was now manifesting itself in cackles of triumphant laughter.

19

Unfortunately, Mrs. Mendlingham's laughter did not stop. Instead, it became that thing most feared in the Devereux by Miss Naismith—an embarrassment. The laughs changed to long, shuddering gasps; ungovernable tears tried to wash out further the washed-out eyes. Mrs. Mendlingham had clearly lost control.

She was manhandled upstairs to her first-floor bedroom by Newth and Colonel Wicksteed. But when laid out on her bed, she did not, as had been hoped, slowly subside into exhausted sleep, so Dr. Ashington was sent for.

He found the old lady in a very disturbed state, talking randomly of disconnected subjects and still intermittently shaken by eruptions of manic laughter.

He managed to sedate her with an injection and then went down to see Miss Naismith.

The proprietress's expression combined grimness (prompted by the lapse of decorum in Mrs. Mendlingham's behaviour) with triumph (prompted by the knowledge that there was now no question but that the old lady would *have to go.*)

Dr. Ashington agreed with this, but said they must move slowly. The threat of removal from the Devereux was, according to her disjointed ramblings, one of the causes of Mrs. Mendlingham's condition. She must be left for a while to sleep off the emotional upheaval of her attack. If she were to awake in the same state, Dr. Ashington said, placing a small medicine bottle on the office desk, she should be given some of this sleeping draught. Two 5 millilitre teaspoonsful in about three times as much water. At not less than four-hour intervals. As was written on the label. It would be dangerous to exceed the stated dose, he cautioned.

Miss Naismith took note of these instructions in a responsible manner and, after Dr. Ashington's departure, produced her calculator from the desk drawer and started to work out new sums, which incorporated a revised price for Mrs. Mendlingham's room as well as the increased rates on Mrs. Selsby's and Miss Wardstone's.

Mrs. Mendlingham did wake in more or less the same state. Mrs. Pargeter, who had just gone upstairs to change for the evening, heard a sudden shriek as she passed the old lady's door, and went inside to find the cause.

Mrs. Mendlingham was bunched up on a huge pile of pillows against the headboard, as if shrinking from something that crawled up the bed towards her. The old eyes were wide with horror.

"It's all right," said Mrs. Pargeter, going across to take the thin hand. "You've just had a bad dream."

This idea was greeted by another wild cackle of laughter. "Not a dream," said Mrs. Mendlingham. "It was real. It happened. I saw it happen."

"What?"

But the gentleness of the enquiry did not deceive the old lady. Her eyes were suddenly intelligent and guarded. "Why should I tell you? Only make trouble if I tell you."

So close to the bed, Mrs. Pargeter's nose could not avoid the conclusion that Mrs. Mendlingham had suffered yet another lapse of continence. Taking the old lady's arm firmly, she said, "Come on, let's get you cleaned up."

Fear came back into the faded eyes. "Oh, no. If Miss Naismith finds out, I'll be—"

"Don't worry."

Mrs. Pargeter pressed the bell by the bed, which after a moment produced Loxton, flustered by an unexpected call at the time she usually allocated to laying the tables for dinner.

"Loxton." Mrs. Pargeter spoke with cool authority. "I'm afraid we've had a bit of an accident. Could you find us some clean sheets, please?"

"Yes, Madam," she replied in her best chambermaid manner, but before she reached the door she was stopped again by Mrs. Pargeter's voice.

"I want these sheets replaced and laundered without Miss Naismith's knowledge."

"Oh, I don't think that would be possible, Madam. Miss Naismith is always most insistent that I should report . . ."

Her words petered out as, in one swift graceful movement, Mrs. Pargeter's hand opened her handbag, withdrew a twenty-pound note and held it out.

"Oh. Well, thank you, Madam. I'll do my best." The twenty-pound note disappeared as quickly into the folds of Loxton's uniform.

"I think you should have a bath," Mrs. Pargeter announced firmly to her charge after the door had closed. Taking no notice of the feeble protests offered, she bundled the old lady into a dressing gown and ushered her across the landing to the bathroom. She ran a hot bath and Mrs. Mendlingham, now docile, got into it.

Mrs. Pargeter went back to the bedroom, where Loxton was just finishing making the bed, and handed over the dirty nightdress. "Could you do that when you do the sheets, please?"

"Yes, Madam."

"Thank you, Loxton."

Mrs. Pargeter got Mrs. Mendlingham out of the bath, dried the frail, slack body, dressed it in a clean nightdress and put it back into the clean bed.

"Now, would you like some food? I could ask for something to be sent up."

The old head shook. "Not hungry."

"Is there anything you want?"

The head shook again and the old eyelids seemed to have difficulty in keeping open.

"No, well, that's fine. More sleep will probably do you as much good as anything. Would you like something to help you sleep? I believe the Doctor left some medicine with Miss Naismith."

There was no response to this suggestion, but Mrs. Pargeter decided it was probably the moment to hand over responsibility, so she went down and found Miss Naismith in the Office.

"Mrs. Mendlingham has woken up. She's still in a fairly confused state. I think it might be a good idea for her to have some of the sleeping draught the Doctor left."

"Thank you, Mrs. Pargeter. It's most thoughtful of you to tell me." Since the accusations of the previous morning, Miss Naismith's manner towards her new resident would now have qualified her for one of the most ticklish of ambassadorial posts. "I will mix the draught for her."

Mrs. Pargeter went back upstairs to complete her original intention and dress for the evening.

Miss Naismith went to the kitchen, carefully measured out two 5 millilitre teaspoonsful of medicine into a tumbler, and added water. She then took this and the medicine bottle upstairs.

Inside Mrs. Mendlingham's room, it seemed that the draught was unnecessary. The old lady lay marooned, slipping a little sideways on her great pile of pillows. From her sagging mouth, deep, regular breaths sounded. Miss Naismith went across to the bedside table and put down the tumbler and the bottle. They might be needed later in the night.

She looked without sentiment at the washed-out face on the pillows, then briskly left the room.

As soon as the door clicked, one eyelid flickered cautiously open. The room was empty. The other eyelid opened. The eyes they revealed were alert, sharp and ill-intentioned.

Reaching under her clean bedclothes, Mrs. Mendlingham produced her hard-covered black notebook and pen.

She started to write.

20

7 MARCH—10:15 p.m.—*It has to be tonight. At the moment I can't tell exactly how much she knows, but with every passing minute the danger of her saying something indiscreet becomes that much greater, so I have to act quickly.*

Besides, let's face it—if I am honest with myself (and that is one thing I have always resolutely tried to be)—I am really looking forward to doing it.

21

At three o'clock in the morning the Devereux was silent except for the constant, almost-forgotten, rhythmic swishing of the sea. Maybe some of the residents snored or grunted in their sleep, but none was so lacking in gentility as to let such noises percolate through a bedroom door on to the second-floor landing where the murderer stood.

The diarist felt heady with suppressed excitement, but completely in control of the situation. It would not, after all, be the first time, and the inquest of the previous day had awarded a seal of approval to the quality of the first murder. Quick, efficient, and without raising a whisper of suspicion. That was the sort of standard that must be maintained in the second murder.

The diarist paused for a long moment outside Mrs. Pargeter's door. She was a meddling woman, the diarist reflected, who showed far too much interest in what went on at the Devereux. There was also a shrewd intelligence there, which might all too quickly make unwelcome connections between apparently irrelevant details. Mrs. Pargeter could be a threat.

The diarist put an ear to the door, and heard the deep, rhythmic breathing of someone at peace with the world. That was ideal. How very convenient.

Then the diarist went down the stairs to the first-floor landing and, for the second time that evening, opened the door of Mrs. Mendlingham's room.

The curtains were imperfectly drawn, and a slice of greyish light fell across the bedside table and the pillows. On the table the level in the medicine bottle showed gratifyingly lower than it had been when Miss Naismith had brought it upstairs the previous evening. The tumbler was empty, another cause for satisfaction.

The stiffening of Mrs. Mendlingham's draught had been the reason for the diarist's first visit to her room that night. The equivalent of fifteen 2 millilitre spoonfuls had been decanted into the tumbler and mixed with the minimum of water. The diarist had anticipated that, as was her custom, the old lady, however strong the sedative, would have woken after a few hours, and turned for comfort to another dose. This was confirmed not only by the empty tumbler, but also by the slow, slow rhythm of the breaths that stirred her body.

The diarist moved forward to the bed and looked down at the old face, around which grey hair sprayed, Medusa-like, onto the pillows. Her position on the bed was very satisfactory, face pressed sideways, almost buried into a pillow.

It was time to remove the "almost" from that burial.

Gingerly, with gloved hands, the diarist lifted the end of the pillow and slowly, slowly moved it up till the surface pressed against the old face.

The body twitched at the discomfort, but was too comatose to make much of a struggle.

The gloved hands exerted a little more pressure, bringing the pillow round to wrap like a gag across the gaping mouth.

The rhythm of the breathing changed to a little choke. The body gave a final twitch of recalcitrance, a final assertion of its atavistic instinct for survival.

But the instincts were too fuddled to co-ordinate the muscles. Sleep, for however long, was more attractive than the efforts of resistance.

Slowly, imperceptibly, the body slumped. With a few small spasms, like those of a child falling asleep, Mrs. Mendlingham sank into oblivion.

The diarist slackened the pressure and checked that there was no more breath. Then, slightly pulling out the trapped end of the pillow, the gloved hands arranged it to flop over the motionless face.

The diarist stood back to assess the handiwork. Good. Artistically satisfying. The pillow lay naturally, as if it had been displaced by the burrowing head and fallen accidentally across the drug-slackened face.

Excellent. Yes, riskier than Mrs. Selsby's death, maybe raising more possibilities for suspicion, but basically another job well done.

The gloved hands were rubbed together with satisfaction.

Then the diarist returned to bed, fell instantly asleep and slept well until the morning.

22

It was at breakfast in the Admiral's Dining Room the next morning that Mrs. Pargeter noticed the absence of Mrs. Mendlingham. The old lady did not like early morning tea, so was not regularly woken by Loxton's seven-thirty knock. Her erratic memory, however, did sometimes make her late for meals and usually, if she hadn't appeared for breakfast by eight-fifteen, Miss Naismith would send Newth up to rap peremptorily on the bedroom door. But on the morning of Friday the 8th of March, in view of the events of the previous day, Miss Naismith did not insist on this. Now that she was confident of soon being rid of Mrs. Mendlingham, she could afford to be magnanimous.

For Mrs. Pargeter the old lady's absence rang an immediate and instinctive alarm bell. Muttering an excuse about having left a handkerchief upstairs, she picked up her handbag, left the Admiral's Dining Room before Loxton had served her kipper, and hurried upstairs.

Inside Mrs. Mendlingham's room, her body lay exactly as the diarist had left it. The brightness of day intensified the light through the curtains, which, though in a bolder stripe across the bed, diffused throughout the room.

Mrs. Pargeter paused inside the door. The stillness of the body, the face hidden by the pillow, both gave her an ugly premonition.

One of the late Mr. Pargeter's useful pieces of advice would have met with Miss Naismith's approval. Any wife of his, he insisted, should at all times carry a pair of gloves in her handbag.

Mrs. Pargeter, obedient to him in all such matters, habitually followed this recommendation, and she put on her gloves before going across to confirm the suspicion, of which she was becoming increasingly certain, that Mrs. Mendlingham was dead.

Carefully, she raised the edge of the pillow. The congested face and the staring bloodshot eyes left no room for doubt.

Mrs. Pargeter let the pillow drop back.

Miss Naismith would have to be informed.

But that could wait for a minute. Mrs. Pargeter moved across to the bedside table and, without touching anything, checked the contents of the bottle and tumbler. The appropriate dosage was clearly written on the label in Dr. Ashington's neat, thin hand; there was no possibility for error. And yet, assuming that the Doctor had handed over a full bottle the previous day, considerably more than the permissible ten 5 millilitre teaspoonsful had disappeared. The viscous dregs at the bottom of the tumbler also suggested a considerably higher density of medicine than the recommended dilution.

Of course, it was possible that Mrs. Mendlingham, in her fuddled state, had overdosed herself from the bottle, which had been so injudiciously left by her bed. It was possible also that the pillow had slipped across her face and suffocated her by accident.

These things were possible, but Mrs. Pargeter, building on the suspicions that she had formed about Mrs. Selsby's death, inclined to another interpretation of what she saw.

She looked around the room. There was something that should have been there that she could not see.

With gloved hands, she opened the drawers of the bureau and the bedside table, but still did not find what she was expecting.

She moved back to the bed, and, very gently, felt under the covers to the right side of the corpse. Triumphantly, she pulled out a hard-covered black notebook.

She checked her watch. She had been out of the Admiral's Dining Room for still only three minutes. She could allow herself another couple before her absence might be noticed.

She opened the book, which was filled with Mrs. Mendlingham's scratchy, uneven writing. It was not exactly a diary, though it did contain descriptions of certain events. In fact, it was a rather sad document, the record of an old lady's fight against failing memory. As Mrs. Mendlingham said, she had tried to fix certain facts in her mind by writing them down, and many of the entries were just statements of information, some of them strangely moving.

The new resident's name is Mrs. Pargeter. Mrs. Pargeter. I must remember that. It's an unusual name, but I must remember it. Getting names wrong is just the sort of thing Miss N. notices and I don't want to give her any more ammunition. I must stay at the Devereux. I don't think I could cope with another move at my age. Mrs. Pargeter. Mrs. Pargeter. I must get it right.

But Mrs. Pargeter had no time to linger sentimentally. She flicked through towards the end of the writing and found the entry she was looking for.

What I saw on the landing keeps coming back to me. It is terrible, my memory's so erratic I sometimes think I dreamed it, but then that comfort is denied me and I know for certain that it really did happen. It haunts me. The pressure to tell someone is enormous. But who? The new resident, Mrs. Pargeter, seems sympathetic, but dare I trust her?

It was almost the last entry in the book. Mrs. Pargeter's face was grim. If only Mrs. Mendlingham had taken the decision to trust her, a life might have been saved.

But it was too late for such thoughts.

With great care, Mrs. Pargeter replaced the notebook under the bedclothes where she had found it.

On the landing she took off her gloves and put them back in her handbag.

Then she went downstairs to tell Miss Naismith about the latest death at the Devereux.

23

Dr. Ashington was instantly summoned. He examined the new corpse and, though his personal opinion veered towards a theory of accidental death, he called in the police. There were elements in the case, his own prescribing for Mrs. Mendlingham, Miss Naismith's possible carelessness in leaving the medicine bottle at the bedside, which might give rise to unfortunate gossip and conjecture unless the death were the subject of an official enquiry.

Miss Naismith was extremely unhappy about the idea of the middle-class peace of the Devereux being shattered by an invasion of policemen, but she could see the logic of Dr. Ashington's decision. There were sufficient cases even in the quality Sunday newspapers (which were the only ones that Miss Naismith was ever *seen* to read) about negligence and downright criminality in the running of private hotels or Homes for her to wish to avoid even a hint of suspicion about the Devereux.

The arrival of the police ensured that Mrs. Mendlingham's death prompted considerably more reaction than that of Mrs. Selsby. Perhaps it would have done, anyway. Mrs. Selsby, after all, had seemed to be fading away for years, while Mrs. Mendlingham had been a much more assertive and controversial figure. Then there were the circumstances of the last few days of her life, the accident with the tea, the summons to Miss Naismith's Office, the wild hysterical attack, the calling of the doctor.

And not to be discounted was the fact that hers was a second death in a very short period. The inquest of the previous day had neatly tied the bow on the closed file of Mrs. Selsby's life, and just when the residents of the Devereux might reasonably expect to be getting back to their normal routine, the pattern had been again disrupted by this new death.

These factors all ensured that there was plenty of discussion that morning in the Seaview Lounge, where the residents awaited their respective summonses to the Schooner Bar, in which the police had set up their temporary headquarters. The police were constantly reassuring; their enquiries, they insisted, were purely routine; it was just that in the case of an unexpected, violent death, such enquiries had to be made.

After Miss Naismith had made the constabulary properly aware of the kind of establishment they were dealing with, of the incredibly high standards of the Devereux, and of the exceptional moral and social qualities of its clientele, Mrs. Pargeter, as discoverer of the body, was politely requested to go to the Schooner Bar.

She was encouraged by sympathetic prompting from one of the two plain-clothes detectives to describe exactly what she had done and seen in Mrs. Mendlingham's bedroom that morning. With a little discreet editing (she did not mention her putting on gloves or discovering the notebook under the bedclothes), Mrs. Pargeter did this helpfully and concisely.

"I gather," said the detective, whose name was Mitford, "that you have only recently taken up residence here . . . ?"

"That's true. Only five days ago."

"And a rather unfortunate five days . . . ?" Detective-Sergeant Mitford ventured.

"Yes. A death every other day so far. Miss Naismith certainly didn't mention that feature of the hotel when I arrived."

It had been a risk, but the broad smile on the detective's face showed that she had taken the right approach. After Miss Naismith's suffocating gentility, he was happy to hear a note of humour.

"So, Mrs. Pargeter, you could hardly be expected to have known the deceased very well . . . ?"

"I'm afraid not."

"Or any of the other residents, come to that . . . ?"

Mrs. Pargeter shook her head apologetically.

"I often find . . ." he began slowly, "that in any sort of investigation of an enclosed community—which is what this is—it's useful to get an outsider's view of the situation. People who've been around for any length of time have their judgement clouded by personal loyalties and rivalries, so it's often difficult to get an accurate picture from them."

Mrs. Pargeter waited to see what would come next.

"All I'm saying is that you are in an ideal position,

having just come to the Devereux, to give us a feeling of what the place is like."

Still she didn't say anything. Another invaluable tip from the late Mr. Pargeter had been that one should never volunteer information unless one wishes to change the direction of a questioner's enquiry. Answer every direct question as truthfully as discretion allows, but never give the answers to unasked questions. It is surprising how many important questions never get asked. (This advice was another expression of the late Mr. Pargeter's philosophy of life, which could be summed up in the following sentence: Be scrupulously honest for as long as you can, and never resort to illegality unless there is truly no alternative.)

"How would you describe the atmosphere here, Mrs. Pargeter?"

"Pretty friendly, on the whole," seemed a fair and balanced reply.

"On the whole . . . ?"

"Yes, on the whole," Mrs. Pargeter agreed, beaming. She wasn't going to give him anything he hadn't earned.

"No evidence of internal dissension? Quarrels, arguments, that sort of thing . . . ?"

"No more than you'd expect in a place like this," she replied evenly. "As you said, I haven't been here long, so perhaps everyone's still on their best behaviour with me."

Detective-Sergeant Mitford nodded, again responding to the note of humour in her voice. He paused before continuing, "But there's nothing you have felt, no tensions, no conflicts, that might lead you to suspect that Mrs. Mendlingham's death was anything other than the accident it appears to be . . . ?"

She was tempted. It would be comforting to share

with someone the unpleasant conjectures that had been shaping in her mind. But, on the other hand, those conjectures were based on the flimsiest of instincts and feelings; she did not think they would stand up to serious scrutiny. Anyway, another of the late Mr. Pargeter's dicta had always been: "If the police arrive, be nice to them. But don't *ask* for trouble by inviting them in."

She feigned ignorance. She wasn't going to volunteer the word "murder." "I'm sorry, Detective-Sergeant. I don't understand what you mean."

"Never mind." He tried another tack. "Did you know that Mrs. Mendlingham kept a sort of notebook?"

"I had seen her writing in one, yes," was her honest reply.

Detective-Sergeant Mitford nodded. "It's a strange book. She recorded all kinds of snippets of information and feelings. Haven't read it all through yet, obviously, just glanced at it, but there is one interesting entry. . . ."

"Oh?"

"She refers to having seen something 'on the landing,' something that upset her. . . . Have you any idea what that might be, Mrs. Pargeter?"

"The only thing I can possibly think of," she replied truthfully, "is that it might be something to do with the death of Mrs. Selsby."

"Oh?"

"Well, I don't know whether you've heard what happened, but Mrs. Selsby was killed falling down the stairs from the first-floor landing. Since Mrs. Mendlingham's bedroom is on that landing, it's possible that she saw Mrs. Selsby fall. And that the memory of that— or perhaps the thought that she should have been able to prevent it—is what was upsetting her."

Detective-Sergeant Mitford nodded with satisfaction.

"Thank you, Mrs. Pargeter. You've been most helpful. And may I say that, with regard to the reference to what Mrs. Mendlingham saw on the landing, we have come to exactly the same conclusion as you have."

Well, perhaps not *exactly* the same, thought Mrs. Pargeter.

24

s Mrs. Pargeter was making her way from the Schoo-
er Bar back to the Seaview Lounge, she was stopped in
er tracks by the sound of raised voices behind the
osed Office door. Discovering a sudden interest in the
eaulieu Motor Museum and the Chalk Pits at Amber-
y, she moved across to the hall table on which such
aflets were always kept, and found that she was able
hear the voices much more clearly.

She quickly identified the speakers as Miss Naismith
nd Mr. Holland. The solicitor was resorting to bluster,
e customary weapon of a weak man trying to get his
oint across.

"... and I don't see how we can possibly keep it quiet
ny longer," he was saying. "Our agreement was that
e should only suppress the information for twenty-

four hours, anyway. That time has passed, more th
passed. And now, under these new circumstances
think the police just have to be told."

"I would really rather we kept the matter confide
tial." Miss Naismith's voice was frosted with authori
"The police are here to conduct an enquiry into t
death of Mrs. Mendlingham. I'm sure they will not wi
to be confused by information about another possi
crime."

"Miss Naismith, I don't think we can any long
pretend we are talking about a 'possible' crime. N
client's jewellery disappeared on the night after h
death, and there has been no sign of it since. Th
sounds to me like a classic definition of a robbery, ar
I have a nasty feeling that the longer we leave t
robbery uninvestigated, the less chance we have of ev
seeing the missing property again."

"Surely the jewellery was insured?"

But Mr. Holland was not to be side-tracked by th
irrelevance. "That is even more reason why the the
should be reported. No insurance company is going
pay up unless the crime has been reported to the poli
within a very short period. They are not charitab
institutions, you know."

"I still find the idea of accusing my guests of th
acutely distasteful."

In the Hall, Mrs. Pargeter smiled grimly.

"You realise what will happen?" Miss Naismith
voice continued. "All my residents' bedrooms will
searched, they will be questioned about their mov
ments at certain relevant periods, they may even hav
their backgrounds investigated. . . ."

"That sounds an excellent idea to me," said M
Holland, belatedly assertive. "Then perhaps we w
stand a chance of recovering the stolen property." Wi

surprising self-knowledge, he added, "I was extremely weak-willed not to insist on that course immediately after the theft was discovered."

"As I say, I'm sure these gentlemen from the police will not be interested. They probably represent a different department."

"I'm sure they will be interested. They're bound to want to get as full a background as possible when they're investigating a suspicious death."

"I wish you wouldn't refer to it as that." Miss Naismith sounded pained.

"I know no other way *to* refer to it. That is what it is. And I am absolutely convinced that we should tell the police about the robbery of Mrs. Selsby's jewels."

Miss Naismith might have been expected also to object to the unadorned use of the word "robbery," but her resistance was at an end. She capitulated. "Very well. The police shall be told."

"Shall I tell them?"

"Certainly not!" she snapped at Mr. Holland. "I am the proprietress of the Devereux, and this responsibility—however distasteful—is mine."

She was not going to better that as an exit line. Mrs. Pargeter moved with discreet speed to the Seaview Lounge and the door had closed behind her, before Miss Naismith emerged, like a galleon in full sail, from the Office.

The police clearly shared Mr. Holland's view that the theft of Mrs. Selsby's jewellery *was* an important matter. Miss Naismith's discreet (but none the less shameful) announcement had come just at the moment when they had more or less decided that Mrs. Mendlingham's death had been an accident, and the prospect of some-

121

thing new to investigate was warmly welcomed by both detectives.

All the hotel's residents and staff were immediately requested to assemble in the Seaview Lounge, where the news of the robbery was broken to them by Miss Naismith, flanked by the two detectives. Though she did her best to make it sound like a minor inconvenience, she could not disguise the fact that there had been a serious breach of the hotel's security. And it did not take long for any of those present to realise the implied slur on the character of one of their number.

The robbery was, as Miss Naismith had realised it would be, a much greater shock to the residents than either of the deaths. (That was the reason why she had tried for so long to keep it from them.) Even if Mrs. Selsby's or Mrs. Mendlingham's deaths had been proved to be murder (and that idea had not been entertained by anyone except Mrs. Pargeter—and, of course, the diarist), the knowledge would not have constituted such a blow to the values of the Devereux.

Theft was such a shameful, lower-class crime. In the mind of Colonel Wicksteed, who probably represented, as much as anyone, the average standards of the residents, theft was a shabby business, on a par with bouncing cheques or not paying gambling debts. It was certainly a resignation issue and, indeed, the Colonel rather regretted the passing of the days when a chap found guilty of stealing would be pointedly told that there was a revolver in the desk drawer and left on his own for an hour or so.

"Under these unfortunate circumstances," announced Detective-Sergeant Mitford, "I am afraid we will have to search the premises. I apologise for the inconvenience, but I would be grateful if you could all stay down here while we do that."

122

"I regret," said Miss Naismith, trying to make up for the diminution of her stature caused by the news of the burglary, "that that will interfere considerably with the preparations for luncheon."

When it was explained that Mrs. Ayling, that day's cook, could not possibly have been on the premises when the theft occurred, she was allowed to return to the kitchen, so at least the gastronomic routine of the residents would not be disrupted.

It was also concluded that, since Miss Naismith had work to do in the Office, and Newth had the lunch tables to lay, they might fulfil these duties, on the strict understanding that they did not attempt to go to their rooms.

Miss Naismith, realising that this condition meant she too was on the list of suspects, made a considerable production out of her martyred exit from the Seaview Lounge.

But that was nothing to the production Eulalie Vance made of her reactions to recent events when the surviving residents were left on their own.

"My God!" she cried, wafting across the room in a blur of shawls. "My God! My God!" She came to rest, with one hand winsomely to her temple. "Was there ever a day like this? First, the *tragic* news of poor, dear Mrs. Mendlingham's death, and then, while we're still *reeling*—but *reeling*—from that, suddenly we're all accused of being jewel thieves!"

"Hardly *all* accused," said Lady Ridgleigh tartly. "I hope no one is suggesting that *I* might have had anything to do with such a thing."

Mr. Dawlish giggled. "I'm afraid that's just what they *are* suggesting."

"What?" she snapped, her eyes wide with horror at the suggestion.

123

"No, no, dear lady." Colonel Wicksteed came i
soothingly to mend the fences his friend had broken.
fear once again it's the clumsiness of the British Polic
Force we have to blame. Fine body of men, I've neve
questioned, but, as ever, tact is not their most strikin
characteristic."

"No," Lady Ridgleigh agreed, a little mollified.

"A frightful, *frightful* thing to happen, though,
Eulalie Vance emoted emptily.

"Oh, shut up!" said Miss Wardstone, whose tolera
tion level of Eulalie was low at the best of times. "Wha
we should be doing is thinking who might have stole
the jewels."

"Work it out for ourselves, you mean? Be our ow
Sherlock Holmeses?" asked Mr. Dawlish enthusiast
cally.

"I say, capital idea!" said the Colonel. Then, affectin
a rather strange voice, he misquoted, " 'Apply m
methods, Watson.' Eh?"

Mr. Dawlish rubbed his hands together. He wa
relishing the game. "Well, since theft is a lower-clas
crime, perhaps that's where we ought to look first."

Colonel Wicksteed couldn't keep up with the speed o
his friend's intellect. "Sorry. Not with you."

"I believe, in detective stories, it's traditional first t
suspect the servants."

Lady Ridgleigh quickly ruled out this idea. "But not a
the Devereux. We are talking about Newth and Loxton
remember. If there were anything lax in the morality o
either, Miss Naismith would not have engaged them."

Though the logic of this assertion might, unde
objective scrutiny, be open to question, they all ac
cepted it. Mr. Dawlish seemed to have had the win
taken out of his sails. "Hmm. That rules out th
lower-class idea."

There was a long silence. Mrs. Pargeter looked rigidly out at the sea, and suppressed a giggle. She knew that the eyes of everyone in the room had just flickered towards her. From Miss Naismith that snobbishness and its assumptions had enraged her; from the residents, it was merely amusing.

"Ye-es." Colonel Wicksteed made a long punctuation out of the word. "Yes. Another approach, of course, would be to think who might have had a motive for stealing the jewels."

"That would be impertinent and in very poor taste!" Lady Ridgleigh snapped down the lid on that idea, too.

"Of course, another thing to do would be to find out who's got a criminal record." Mr. Dawlish giggled at the incongruity of his suggestion, incidentally rescuing the Colonel from Lady Ridgleigh's displeasure in the same way that his friend had earlier rescued him.

"Yes," agreed Colonel Wicksteed. "Yes. Damned funny idea."

Once again there was silence while they thought about this. Once again, still staring out to sea in amusement, Mrs. Pargeter felt their eyes on her.

Oh no, she thought. You may inadvertently have got nearer the truth than you realise, but there's no criminal record. The late Mr. Pargeter was far too careful, and Arnold Justiman far too skilful, for that to have happened.

25

The police search of the Devereux for Mrs. Selsby's jewels revealed nothing. Nor did questioning the hotel's staff and residents give them any clue as to where the stolen property might be. Eventually, in the afternoon, they left to file their reports on the two incidents.

Though the official decision on Mrs. Mendlingham's death would have to await a full post-mortem and the findings of a coroner, the police who had gone to the hotel were in no doubt that it had been an unfortunate accident. Miss Naismith might perhaps be reprimanded for the carelessness of leaving a full bottle of sleeping draught within reach of an old lady on the edge of senility, but there was no question in their minds of any criminal activity.

With regard to the other case, as well, the police were

critical of Miss Naismith. By delaying the announcement of the theft (for whatever delicate reasons), she had made their investigation of the incident doubly difficult. The sooner the police can be on the scene of a crime, the greater their chances of solving it. In this instance, the thief had had two days to remove the booty from the premises, which was bound to be his or her first priority, considering the value of the property involved. Since the detailed search of the hotel had revealed nothing, it was reasonable to assume that the jewellery was now in some other safe hiding place.

Mrs. Pargeter did not agree with this conclusion. She felt fairly confident that the stolen property was still in the Devereux.

But then, of course she knew considerably more about Mrs. Selsby's jewellery than the police did.

During the rest of the day she thought about the theft. Though she was convinced that Mrs. Mendlingham's death had been a second murder, that crime took a lower priority in her scheme of investigation.

The second murder had been an inevitable consequence of the first. Mrs. Pargeter could have kicked herself for her stupidity; she had not interpreted Mrs. Mendlingham's ramblings correctly. When the old lady had appeared upset by what she had seen "on the landing," Mrs. Pargeter had read that as an expression of a guilty conscience. She had assumed that Mrs. Mendlingham was making an oblique confession to having been the one who pushed Mrs. Selsby down the stairs.

Whereas now, as her own murder had shown, what had really been upsetting the old lady had been the fact that she had witnessed *someone else* pushing Mrs. Selsby down the stairs. It was this that had prompted the anguished comments in her notebook. Unfortunately, she had somehow communicated what she had seen to Mrs. Selsby's murderer and, of course, from that moment, had signed her own death warrant.

So, although Mrs. Pargeter wanted to identify Mrs. Mendlingham's murderer, she concentrated on Mrs. Selsby's death. Even though she did not yet understand the motivation for the crime, she felt certain that the theft of the jewellery was in some way relevant.

The excitements of the morning had taken their toll on the residents of the Devereux, and there was a general feeling that the afternoon should be a time for private recuperation, so that they could all meet for tea in a better state to maintain the polite fiction that nothing had happened. Displays of emotion (except for the vacuous posturings of Eulalie Vance, which everyone ignored) were as little welcomed in the Devereux as midday baths, so an upheaval of the kind they had all experienced must inevitably be followed by a period of solitary rehabilitation.

The residents approached this task in different ways. Colonel Wicksteed swept Mr. Dawlish off for a "brisk walk" with the irrelevant misquotation that "the rolling drunken Englishman made the English rolling road." Lady Ridgleigh and Miss Wardstone went up to their rooms for a "lie-down," and Eulalie Vance, as Mrs. Pargeter discovered when she went in there round half-past three, snored gently in her armchair in the Seaview Lounge.

Mrs. Pargeter looked out at the relentlessly grey sea and focused her mind on the theft of Mrs. Selsby's jewels. The timing of the crime was interesting and, along with other factors, seemed to rule out a financial motive. If someone in the Devereux had wished to steal the jewellery merely to sell it, then they would have done better to commit the theft at any other time. Mrs. Selsby's room would frequently have been left unlocked and, given her age and short sight, it was possible that the loss of the jewellery would not have been discovered straight away. The thief would have had time to dispose of it as and when he or she thought fit.

But committing the crime the night after her death meant that it was bound to be quickly discovered. Only a fool would make such a theft then for the conventional profit motive; and Mrs. Pargeter was increasingly certain that she was not dealing with a fool.

Which meant that the motive for the theft could not be simply financial.

In her mind she went round the hotel, room by room. The police, in their search, had concentrated on places where valuables might be safely hidden, but that wasn't at all what Mrs. Pargeter was looking for in her mental tour of the premises.

From somewhere in the depths of the hotel came a faint scraping noise. Newth raking out the boiler. Mrs. Pargeter was beginning to recognise the background sounds of the Devereux, the rhythms of the hotel's life, the ticking of the grandfather clock, all the creaks and judders of the old building. She could understand how, in time, these noises could prove very soothing, very peaceful for a long-term resident.

Eulalie Vance woke with a little snort and looked around her in bewilderment. "Oh, dear me," she said. "Couldn't think where I was for a moment. Thought it was morning."

Mrs. Pargeter smiled benignly at the former actress. How kind, you've given me just the lead I need, she thought, as the door of the Seaview Lounge opened and the surviving residents started to assemble for afternoon tea.

26

he was getting quite used to nocturnal expeditions,
nd rather welcomed them. She found they brought
ack some of the excitements of the life she had shared
vith the late Mr. Pargeter.

In the course of her marriage she had had to train
erself to wake at a given hour in the night, do
vhatever was necessary, then return to bed and go
traight back to sleep. It was a useful skill.

That night she woke obediently at three, and lay still
or a few moments, thinking what she had to do. Eulalie
ad given her the clue by thinking it was morning when
he awoke. Had Mrs. Pargeter been longer at the
Devereux, she too would have become aware of the
egularity with which Newth raked out the boiler every

morning, and she too would have got into the habit of waking to that distant scraping sound.

It followed that for Newth to be cleaning out the boiler in the middle of the afternoon was unusual, and in an institution as bound by routine as the Devereux there must be a reason for anything unusual.

The police would not have looked in the boiler for the jewels. Only in a moment of panic would a conventional thief have put them there, and between the announcement of the theft and the end of the search there had been no opportunity for the thief, however panicked, to attempt to destroy the evidence.

But, as Mrs. Pargeter had recognised, she was not dealing with a conventional thief or a conventional theft.

She knew she could not go down the main staircase. The pressure pads in the Hall would activate the alarms. But in her investigation of the hotel's security system she had observed that there were no pressure pads at the back of the ground floor. There, presumably so that there was no danger of Newth's triggering the system when he started his early morning routine, the burglar alarms were linked just to contact breakers on the exterior doors. This meant that Mrs. Pargeter could go safely down the back stairs towards the kitchen, and although she had not been down to check, she was assuming that she would be equally safe on the next flight down to the basement.

She put her dressing gown on over her nightdress and donned soft sheepskin slippers. She had contemplated more suitable clothes for investigation of the boiler room, but decided that their advantages were outweighed by the problems of explanation that might be caused if she were interrupted in her mission. An old lady wandering around at three a.m. in her night clothes could be put down to the aberrations of age; an old lady in a dark sweater and trousers might raise more searching questions.

She put the late Mr. Pargeter's skeleton keys and pencil torch in her dressing-gown pocket and left her bedroom. On the landing the night safety light glowed weakly. Mrs. Pargeter moved along the corridor past the bathrooms to the back stairs. She stepped, as the late Mr. Pargeter had taught her, on the balls of her feet, allowing her full weight to descend slowly with each footfall, alert to the beginnings of any creak in the floorboards.

She wafted in ghost-like silence to the ground floor. There was no light there, but she could see to locate the door down to the basement. No point in taking unnecessary risks by switching on a light.

On the stairs to the basement, because of their unfamiliarity, she used the pencil torch, directing its beam, as the late Mr. Pargeter had instructed her, exactly where she was about to place each foot. She heard the subdued roar of the boiler as she drew closer to it.

At the foot of the stairs was a small area off which two doors opened. One would be Newth's bedsitter and the other the boiler room. She listened for a moment at Newth's door, and heard only reassuringly heavy breathing. Then, pulling the handle firmly towards her to stop any telltale rattling (as the late Mr. Pargeter had also instructed her), she opened the door to the boiler room.

A predictable blast of hot air greeted her, and her slippered foot scrunched on coke dust. Though she ran the risk of slowing her exit, she closed the door behind her to minimise noise.

She beamed the pencil torch round the room, quickly

taking in its dimensions. The old iron boiler, through a small grille of which a sullen red light glowed, dominated the space. To one side of it was a boarded-off area half-filled with a high slope of coke; above this a trap door through which the fuel was dropped. A shovel and some blackened buckets stood in front of the pile. A small heavily bolted door, which also showed the signs of a contact-breaking burglar alarm, led off the room, presumably to the yard outside.

Mrs. Pargeter was a little disappointed. She had hoped to see a pile of clinker, a sort of half-way house where the boiler's debris would rest before being taken outside, but Newth was too organised for that. No, when he cleared out the ash-tray beneath the boiler, he took the clinker straight out to the bins or wherever else it was that he disposed of it.

So, if, as she had planned, Mrs. Pargeter was to examine what had been raked out that afternoon, she would have to wait till the exposure of daylight or risk the burglar alarms.

She stood for a moment, undecided, then moved across towards the buckets. The crunching underfoot sounded hideously loud, but she rationalised that it was unlikely to be heard above the steady, regular roar of the boiler.

She directed her torch down to the buckets. Again she was disappointed. Maybe she had hoped to find them still loaded with the afternoon's clinker, but she was out of luck. The buckets were empty; only dust and ash clung to their battered sides.

She checked her watch. Probably time to go back. Minimise risks. Try another tack, in the morning.

She gave a final sweep with her torch to the inside of the buckets and was stopped by a dull flash from inside one of them. She brought the torch down nearer and

aw the satisfying gleam of a droplet of metal clinging to
ae side.

It must have spattered there while still molten, and
lung to the side when the hot ash was cleared. Mrs.
argeter leant down and prised the little sliver of metal
)ose with her finger-nail. She popped it into her
ressing-gown pocket and left the boiler room as quietly
s she had arrived.

Inside a minute she was back in her bedroom. She
witched on the light and placed the scrap of metal on
tissue on her dressing table. She got out the late Mr.
argeter's eye-glass and peered down at her trophy.

There was no doubt about it. During her not unevent-
ıl life with her late husband, Mrs. Pargeter had seen
nough melted-down pieces of metal like that to
ecognise it instantly.

It was a cheap alloy, silver-plated.

And on its surface was still the blurred outline of a
racery design.

Which she recognised as part of the setting of one of
Mrs. Selsby's necklaces.

And it confirmed Mrs. Pargeter's conjecture that all of
he old lady's jewellery had been destroyed in the boiler
f the Devereux Hotel.

27

It had been a long five days at the Devereux, with more excitement than was normally rationed out to the hotel over as many years. The arrival of one new resident would usually have provided enough gossip-fodder for five months, and yet as well as that there had been the deaths of two other residents, visitation by the police, and—more shocking than all of these—a robbery. It was sincerely hoped that they would all have a quiet weekend.

Saturday, Mrs. Pargeter had discovered, was Newth's day off. While for most hotels the weekend was the busiest period, this was not the case at the Devereux, because all of its guests stayed on a semipermanent basis. Indeed, often the weekends were less busy than the weekdays, as some of the residents might go off to stay with friends or surviving relatives.

So Newth was free from the moment he finished his breakfast routine on the Saturday (usually about nine) until twelve o'clock the next day, when he was expected to be back to help with Sunday lunch. In theory he could go anywhere he liked during that period, though in practice he always came back to the hotel to sleep on the Saturday night.

That morning Mrs. Pargeter breakfasted quickly and was out of the Admiral's Dining Room even before Colonel Wicksteed had had time to make his remark about time and tide. She put on her mink and left the hotel. She walked briskly some fifty metres along the front, then turned up a road leading into the town. In her tour of Littlehampton on the Tuesday, amongst other essential services, she had located a garage that operated a car rental service.

This garage, she had observed, opened for business at eight-thirty. By ten to nine she was parked on the sea front a little way away from the Devereux at the wheel of a brand-new Vauxhall Cavalier.

Newth emerged from a side entrance promptly at nine. He was pushing a motor scooter, which he mounted and drove off at a sedate pace along the coast road towards Worthing.

He was unaware of the Vauxhall Cavalier driving sedately behind him. There was, after all, nothing unusual about it. The roads of the South Coast are heavily populated by beautifully polished cars that never exceed the speed of a motor scooter. (Most of them, incidentally, have sunshine roofs and are driven by balding men in cravats and string-backed driving gloves, but that's neither here nor there.)

Mrs. Pargeter did not know where she was expecting her quarry to go, but, after her discovery of the night before, anything Newth did might be significant.

The evidence of the metal from the boiler room made her almost certain that he was responsible for the robbery from Mrs. Selsby's room. It made sense that that crime should have been committed by a member of staff. There had been no sign of forcible entry to the room, and, though she couldn't think that many of the residents would have sets of skeleton keys like the late Mr. Pargeter's, she knew that the staff had pass keys. That fact, combined with the use of the boiler as a means of destruction, seemed to point the finger very firmly at Newth.

Whether he was acting for himself or on someone else's behalf, she had not yet decided. It was clear that Newth had a special status in the hotel. He certainly did things for Miss Naismith that were outside the scope of the job for which he was employed, and it was possible that he had comparable arrangements with some of the residents. He carried about him the discreet aura of a factotum, and Mrs. Pargeter had the feeling that, presented with the appropriate amount of money, there was no service he would refuse to perform.

She had not yet worked out whether Newth's guilt in the matter of the robbery also made him a suitable candidate for the role of murderer. The crimes were certainly linked, but the link might not be so direct. Mrs. Pargeter would bide her time, and gather more information, before she formed an opinion on that.

The motor scooter continued its unhurried course eastwards along the coast. The Vauxhall Cavalier pottered along behind. Sometimes a few vehicles came between them, but Mrs. Pargeter never let Newth out of her sight.

He drove through Worthing, still keeping as near to he sea as possible, and on into the bungaloid sprawl of Lancing. Here at last he turned inland. Mrs. Pargeter, ulled into inattention by the predictability of his course, almost overshot the turning and had to brake sharply to follow.

She didn't have far to go. A little way up the road, Newth turned again on to the muddy road of a new development. It appeared to be a cul-de-sac, so, rather than following him in, Mrs. Pargeter brought the Cavalier to a halt on the other side of the road a little way from the entrance. She could still see Newth clearly as he slowed down and parked the motor scooter.

She reached into the glove compartment for the late Mr. Pargeter's small but very powerful binoculars. There was nobody about, so she was not worried about raising them to her eyes and focusing on the neat military figure across the road.

The building site was, as the sign outside the entrance boasted, "an exclusive development of luxury bungalows," which looked to be nearing completion. The buildings were large and well appointed, all set in generous gardens and boasting double garages. Mrs. Pargeter, who had done an extensive survey of South Coast property before deciding to move into the Devereux, could price the bungalows very accurately. And the price she arrived at was high.

Which made what Newth was doing all the more interesting.

Although it was a Saturday, there were still a lot of men working on the site.

Newth had walked up what would in time be the garden path of the bungalow outside which he had parked, and instantly fallen into conversation with the two men working on the garage doors. They seemed to

recognise him and even show him a degree of deference. They pointed out various features of the house
and then took him inside, presumably to show him
more.

Newth's manner and reactions to what he was shown
could only be described as proprietorial. He behaved
exactly like someone who was buying a new house
and had come along to check the progress of his
acquisition.

This gave Mrs. Pargeter food for thought. Newth
certainly did not have the look of a rich man, nor did the
nature of his employment suggest that he was in a
position to make that kind of investment. Of course, he
might have private money or he might have saved
assiduously through his life, but Mrs. Pargeter didn't
favour either of those explanations.

Nor could the purchase of such a house be the result
of his benefits from Mrs. Selsby's death. Even if he had
known the unusual provisions of her will beforehand,
he couldn't have raised money on that expectation.

There was just no way that the luxury bungalow
fitted the image of a hotel porter.

Perhaps living so long with the late Mr. Pargeter had
made her over-suspicious of people whose life-style was
at odds with their known income, but Mrs. Pargeter felt
pretty convinced that Newth was, at some level or
other, on the fiddle.

Just as she reached this conclusion, he emerged from
the front of the house. Again his manner with the two
builders was excessively bonhomous, almost to the
point of being condescending. It was the manner of
someone in charge; it did not match the silent obsequi-
ousness that he demonstrated around the Devereux.

He started back towards the motor scooter and, since
he was now looking in her direction, Mrs. Pargeter

picked up the newspaper she had bought for the purpose and raised it to her face.

Over the top of the paper, she saw something remarkable happen.

Newth suddenly clutched his chest, stumbled and fell.

He hadn't tripped over anything; his muscles just seemed to have given way. As he slumped to the ground, the two builders rushed forwards to grab his arms. One of them laid him flat on the ground, while the other hurried to the Portakabin in the middle of the site, and returned a moment later with a plastic beaker, presumably full of water or tea.

By the time the man got back, Newth was sitting up and appeared to be protesting vigorously that he was all right. Grudgingly, at the builders' insistence, he took a drink from the beaker; but in spite of their remonstrances, he immediately stood up and walked about, as if to demonstrate his fitness. Mrs. Pargeter watched the dumb show continue, as the builders questioned whether he was all right to drive and whether they should call a doctor, while Newth protested that it was nothing and that he was as right as rain.

At last the builders realised there was nothing they could do to break his determination, so they withdrew and let him return to the scooter. As he mounted it, he waved and called out some over-hearty remark, of which Mrs. Pargeter caught the end. ". . . and keep up the good work. I'll be along to check how you're doing next week. Remember, the sooner I can get in, the happier I'll be."

Which seemed to confirm that he had bought the bungalow. Mrs. Pargeter was more intrigued than ever as to where he had got the money.

The Vauxhall Cavalier followed the motor scooter discreetly and sedately back the way they had come. Mrs. Pargeter drove at first in some trepidation, constantly expecting Newth to have another attack and fall off.

But it didn't happen. He drove safely back to the Devereux. Once inside, he went straight to his bedsitter.

Mrs. Pargeter kept her hire-car parked near the hotel, ready to follow if he decided to take another excursion. But he didn't. He stayed in the bedsitter all day. At half-past six Mrs. Pargeter saw Loxton taking a supper tray down there and was told that Newth was "a bit off-colour—nothing serious, just not a hundred per cent."

And that evening after dinner, while some of the others played bridge and she appeared to read in the Seaview Lounge, Mrs. Pargeter mulled over the new facts she had found out about Newth: first, that he was a rich man, and, second, that he was a sick man.

Oh, yes, and third—that he was almost definitely a thief.

28

9 MARCH—9:30 p.m.—*Well, what an exciting life I seem to be leading! Not only can I now call myself a double murderer, I have even had the police taking notice of my humble efforts. Quite a shock that was, when I heard that they'd been called in. And yet, like many of the other excitements I have undergone since I started on my recent course, it was not wholly unpleasureable. Indeed, after a life of almost unbelievable dullness, I seem to get quite a thrill out of living dangerously.*

I also gain considerable satisfaction from the ignorance of everyone else at the Devereux. They behave to me exactly as they always have, and I think I can congratulate myself on my acting for behaving as I always have. I wish I had realised earlier the pleasures of leading a double life!

Because, in the last few days, partly perhaps because of the evidence of others' mortality (which I have caused), I have become increasingly aware that my own time is getting short. And this thought has caused an interesting change in my attitude to my murders. Only last week I was unworried by the prospect of arrest and conviction—I just thought it might add to the excitement. But now, perhaps because I've seen the police come so close, I am very determined not to get caught.

A new element has entered my life—call it the thrill of the chase, perhaps, or the appeal of a game of cat and mouse—but, whatever it is, I am determined to get away with my crimes, even if—as poor Mrs. Mendlingham found out—this means committing more murders.

In other words, anyone who I find has got near to the truth of what I have done is lining themselves up to be my next victim. The trouble is, I am beginning to develop quite a taste for murder.

29

Mrs. Pargeter decided that she had got as far as she could in her investigation without enlisting outside help. Among the many invaluable legacies of the late Mr. Pargeter had been his address book and, though she had rarely had occasion to use it, she knew it to be a wonderfully rich alternative Yellow Pages, which offered access to a wide variety of unexpected services.

She decided it would be unwise to use one of the telephones at the Devereux, since they all went through the hotel switchboard and she did not wish to have her conversation overheard. So, round ten on the Sunday morning, Mrs. Pargeter set out with a pocketful of change towards the public phone boxes she had located on her day of reconnaissance.

The curtain of grey cloud had parted to let through a

little grudging sunlight. The seaweed smell was strong. Mrs. Pargeter breathed deeply. She felt good, healthy in body and with her mind intriguingly occupied.

Although it had been over five years since they had spoken, she was in no doubt as to whom she should ring, but initially she met with disappointment.

"I'm sorry," said a woman's voice at the other end. "I'm afraid Mr. Hollingberry doesn't live here any more."

"Oh. You don't mean that he's . . . away for a while but will be back?" asked Mrs. Pargeter discreetly.

The woman had obviously never had a relative in prison, because she did not appear to understand the question. "No, no, he's moved."

"Do you have a number for him at his new address?"

She was in luck. The woman gave her the number and Mrs. Pargeter dialed it.

"Hello," said an excessively cultured voice when the money went in. "Bishop's Palace."

Mrs. Pargeter's instinct was to say, "Sorry, wrong number," and put the phone down, but something held her back. "Oh. Er, I wanted to speak to a Mr. Hollingberry."

"Just a moment, I'll call him to the telephone."

There was a wait of nearly a minute and then a familiar voice said, "Good morning. Can I help you?"

"Kipper?"

"Yes. Who is this?"

"It's Melita Pargeter."

"Mrs. Pargeter! Oh, what a pleasure to hear your voice, Madam. May I say, Madam, that I think of you a great deal. You and, of course, poor Mr. Pargeter. I know it's been over five years since he passed on, but I do find I still miss him, you know."

"Yes," said Mrs. Pargeter wistfully. "I know." Then,

146

warding off introspection, she asked, "What on earth are you doing in a Bishop's Palace?"

"I work here," Kipper Hollingberry replied with dignity.

"Oh?"

"I am his Lordship's chauffeur."

"I didn't know that was your line of country, Kipper."

"I have always," he said rather primly, "aspired to the quiet of a Cathedral Close. That is where I always wished to spend my later years. An ambition perhaps deriving from an early affection for the works of Trollope."

"Oh. Well, perhaps if you've changed direction so completely, you won't be able to help me. . . ."

"Mrs. Pargeter, I would always help you. I can never forget yours and Mr. Pargeter's kindness to me on so many occasions. Any service to repay a little of my debt of gratitude I will gladly perform."

"I know that, Kipper. I was only thinking that, now you're out of the swing, you probably won't have the information I require."

"I am by no means 'out of the swing,' Madam."

"What, you're still in business?"

"In a smaller way. My service is now, let's say . . . a consultancy."

"And you run it from the Bishop's Palace?"

"Yes. Only for selected clients, of course."

"Hmm. You've still got the Directory?"

"Certainly. And I pride myself on keeping the information in it right up to date."

The pips went. Mrs. Pargeter put in more money.

"Give me the number," said Kipper. "Next time that happens I'll call you back."

"What about the Bishop's telephone bill?"

"His Lordship trusts me implicitly." There was a note of reproof in Kipper's voice. "Now what can I do for you?"

"It's a safe."

"Yes?" he sounded unsurprised. "What make?"

"Clissold & Fry—Excalibur Two."

"Hmm. They're pretty straightforward. Plastic explosives. Doesn't need much, they're not very robust."

"No, no. I don't want any sign that it's been opened."

"Ah. Combination job. Right."

"That's the sort of information you'd have on the Directory, isn't it?"

"Should do, certainly. Depend a bit when the safe was sold. My contact at Clissold & Fry got, er, a little careless. I'm afraid he's been . . . um, away for the last three years and I haven't as yet been able to replace him. But, if it's more than three years ago, I'll have copies of the lot . . . sales invoice, combination."

"I should think it probably has been there three years. Doesn't look very new."

"Well, where is the safe?"

"The Devereux Hotel, South Terrace, Littlehampton."

"Any idea of the name of the purchaser?"

"The current proprietress's name is Miss Naismith."

"Splendid. I'll check it out for you, Madam."

"How long's it likely to take, Kipper?"

"Five minutes maximum. Shall I call you back on that number?"

"If you wouldn't mind."

"Of course not. I must say, Mrs. Pargeter, it's a real tonic to hear from you again. And I'm delighted to be able to help you. Even a tiny thing like this. Please remember, if there's ever anything more I can do for you . . . you know, anything bigger . . . don't hesitate to ask."

"That's very kind of you, Kipper."

"My pleasure. Not that I wouldn't have done it anyway, but you know, before he went, Mr. Pargeter asked me to look after you, help out if you ever needed anything."

"Oh. I didn't know that."

"Well, he did. He was a good man, Mr. Pargeter."

"Yes."

"I'll ring you back."

After she had put the phone down, Mrs. Pargeter allowed herself the rare indulgence of a tear. It was true, he had been a good man. How many widows, she wondered, were as well looked after in such varied, unexpected ways?

Kipper Hollingberry rang back two and a half minutes later.

"Invoice dated the seventh of May 1975."

"Quite a long time ago."

"Thought it would be. That Excalibur's pretty out of date, been superseded."

"And have you got the combination?"

"Of course," said Kipper, and gave her the number.

30

When she got back to the Devereux, she was interested to see a red Porsche parked untidily outside the main entrance. As soon as she entered the Schooner Bar just after twelve for a pre-lunch drink, she was introduced to its owner.

Though the word "introduce" was perhaps inadequate to describe the production Lady Ridgleigh made of showing off the young man with her to the Devereux's newest resident.

"Mrs. Pargeter," she gushed, "I don't believe you've had the pleasure of meeting my son, Miles."

"No, I haven't. How do you do?"

The young man who took her hand was tall like his mother, but in him the bony outline took on an adolescent gawkiness, which was at odds with his receding gingerish hair and the tight nets of lines around his pale blue eyes. He must have been at least thirty-five.

"How do you do? Delighted to meet you." His voice had the vacuous resonance of a public-school education not backed up by native intelligence.

"Can I get you a drink?"

His hand moved towards the inside pocket of his blazer, but it was a half-hearted gesture, like that of the average husband offering to help with the washing-up; it expected to be stopped.

And indeed it was. Lady Ridgleigh came in smartly on her cue. "No, no, Miles, please. Down here you're my guest."

"Oh, very well, old thing," he said, conceding without even the pretence of a struggle.

Lady Ridgleigh reached into a crocodile-skin handbag, produced a monogrammed purse and gave Newth the order. She was drinking a Martini, Mrs. Pargeter noticed, wondering whether this was a regular Sunday indulgence or just in honour of her visitor.

The visitor in question took a long swill from his pint of beer, winced, and gave Mrs. Pargeter a weak smile.

"Irrigating the old system, you know. Got a bit châteaued last night. Some damned hop at the Grosvenor House. When will I ever learn?" he asked in the voice of someone who had no intention of ever learning.

"Your car outside, is it?" asked Mrs. Pargeter.

"The old Porky Porsche? Yes. Goes all right, this one."

"You mean you've got more than one?"

Miles Ridgleigh guffawed. "That'll be the day. No, I've *had* more than one, though. Have a nasty habit of wrapping them round lamp-posts—don't I, Mums?"

He appealed to his mother for approbation and was

rewarded by an indulgent "boys will be boys" smile. Lady Ridgleigh was totally transformed by her son's presence. She looked radiant, almost skittish. She beamed fatuously like a young girl in love. Mrs. Pargeter wondered whether this was how she had behaved in the company of the late lamented Froggie. She thought, on balance, it was unlikely.

"You work in London, then, do you, Miles?"

This suggestion was greeted by another empty guffaw. "Well, I *live* in London, anyway. Most of my chums are up there. Though, as you see, I'm not above coming down to the old Costa Geriatrica to do the dutiful son bit."

Lady Ridgleigh looked disproportionately grateful for this magnanimity.

Mrs. Pargeter watched Miles continuing to do his "dutiful son bit" throughout Sunday lunch. It seemed to consist largely of telling loud, unresolved anecdotes and of drinking a great deal. The Ridgleighs had two bottles of wine with the meal, and the mother could not have drunk more than a couple of glasses.

With coffee in the Seaview Lounge Miles downed a couple of hasty brandies, then rose abruptly and announced, "Got to be off, old thing. Promised to drop in on some chums Haywards Heath way."

Lady Ridgleigh's face dropped. Clearly she had not expected this exquisite visit to be so suddenly curtailed.

But Miles either didn't notice or ignored her expression. "So got to dash. But don't worry, I'll be down again soon to salve the old social conscience."

"Oh, well, Miles—"

"Not a word of thanks. Won't hear of it, old thing. My pleasure." Then his tone changed. "Perhaps you'd like to *see me out* . . . ?"

The intonation on the last words clearly had some private meaning for them both.

"Oh. Oh yes," said Lady Ridgleigh, and started for the door.

"Mustn't forget this, must we?" Miles lifted up her crocodile handbag with what was almost a leer.

"No. No. Of course not."

It was nearly five minutes before Miles could be seen from the windows of the Seaview Lounge approaching his Porsche. Mrs. Pargeter felt fairly sure that she knew the nature of the transaction that had delayed him.

With a cheery wave, he folded his long body into the driving seat, and the Porsche scorched off erratically down South Terrace.

But Mrs. Pargeter soon forgot about Miles Ridgleigh. As she seemed to read the Sunday papers, she thought about what she had to do.

It would have to be another middle-of-the-night mission, she decided. There were too many people in and out of the Hall during the day for her to risk going into the Office then. So she continued to read the Sunday papers, ate a large tea and a light supper, played Scrabble in the evening with Eulalie Vance, and contained her excitement.

If the Office safe yielded what she hoped, it would represent the most significant advance since she had started her investigation.

Mrs. Pargeter went to bed at half-past ten, programming herself to wake four hours later.

31

The routine was by now familiar. She got out of bed, put on her dressing gown, gloves and sheepskin slippers. In her pockets she put the late Mr. Pargeter's skeleton keys, pencil torch and eye-glass. Then she slipped out on to the landing.

She was now accustomed to the creaky stairs of the main flights and avoided them expertly. She glanced at the other residents' bedroom doors as she went down, but all appeared to be safely closed. When she reached the Entrance Hall, the door down to Newth's domain was also shut.

She trod gently in the Hall, although she had checked that there were no pressure pads except in front of the main doors. During the day, she had taken an unobtrusive look at the lock on the Office door and she had the right skeleton key ready.

It slipped in and turned silently as if it had been cut specifically for that lock. Mrs. Pargeter went inside and closed the Office door behind her.

She switched on the late Mr. Pargeter's torch and moved across to the safe. She memorised the exact setting of the dials and then her gloved fingers expertly twiddled them to the numbers Kipper Hollingberry had provided. The safe door swung open easily and silently.

There was quite a lot of money on the top shelf, piles of large denomination notes held by rubber bands, but she ignored this. She also ignored her own jewellery, and homed in on a pile of jewel cases on the bottom shelf.

She took them out of the safe and saw with satisfaction that on the top of each Lady Ridgleigh's monogram was impressed in gold.

She removed the contents of the first box, matching necklace, bracelet and ear-rings of emeralds set in silver. She examined these minutely with the late Mr. Pargeter's eye-glass.

She replaced them and moved on to the next box. An opal necklace. This was subjected to the same intense scrutiny.

She thought she heard a noise and froze. The irreverent thought occurred to her that to be discovered now would not be good for her image. If Miss Naismith wanted confirmation of the suspicions she had had about the theft of Mrs. Selsby's jewellery . . .

There was no further noise. Perhaps she'd imagined it.

She continued to work through all of Lady Ridgleigh's jewellery. When she had finished, with a little sigh of satisfaction, she replaced the boxes on the bottom shelf exactly as she had found them. She closed the safe door and reset the dials exactly as they had been before. Then she left the Office and carefully relocked the door.

She felt euphoric as she returned silently to her room. She had been right.

The settings of Lady Ridgleigh's jewellery were real silver and gold. But all of the stones were well-made imitations.

Just as all of Mrs. Selsby's had been.

So euphoric was she, so delighted to have had her suspicion proved right, that Mrs. Pargeter did not look around on her way from the Entrance Hall up to her bedroom on the second floor.

So she did not notice a door opened a crack, or see through it the gleam of the diarist's eye.

32

Mrs. Pargeter woke at seven-thirty the next morning and lay luxuriously in bed, feeling pleased with herself. The revelation about Lady Ridgleigh's jewels had cleared an obstruction in the logic of her thinking about the crimes at the Devereux Hotel.

She had known for some time why Mrs. Selsby's jewels had been stolen the night after her murder. When she had examined them just before the theft, she had seen that they were all fakes. According to Mr. Holland, Mrs. Selsby had plenty of money, so she was unlikely to have made the substitution herself. But she was a short-sighted old lady and would not have been able to tell the false stones and settings from real ones. The copies had been well done, and Mrs. Pargeter wasn't certain whether she herself would have been able to tell they were imitations without her late husband's eye-glass.

So someone other than Mrs. Selsby had made the substitution. It was quite a neat crime, given a wealthy absent-minded old lady who was in the habit of leaving her jewellery lying around. All the criminal had to do was to borrow one item at a time, take it to a specialist in such work, and have a replica made. The expertise would no doubt be expensive, but a small investment compared to the resale value of the stolen jewels. The item would then be returned before its owner had missed it, and Mrs. Selsby would have been far too short-sighted to realise that anything had changed. The crime could then be repeated at will for as long as the jewellery lasted.

But with Mrs. Selsby's death, suddenly the doctored jewellery became incriminating evidence, which had to be removed and destroyed. One of the first actions of a Mr. Holland (or whoever else might be appointed to look after the old lady's affairs) would be to have the jewellery valued. And it would take a skilled jeweller a matter of seconds to recognise the fakes. Then very unpleasant enquiries might ensue.

Realising this, the criminal must have decided that, since some sort of enquiry was inevitable, an investigation of a straightforward robbery would be the safest. Theft of valuable items was a commonplace crime. The thief could not have predicted that Miss Naismith's gentility would delay the announcement of the robbery, but, even without that bonus, he or she was safe in assuming that a police search would concentrate on places where valuable objects might be protected, rather than where worthless objects might be destroyed.

It was only because she had examined the jewels

before the theft that Mrs. Pargeter had been able to make this leap of logic and search the boiler room.

That, then, was the crime. The question that remained was: Who had perpetrated it?

Mrs. Pargeter still felt convinced it was Newth. He had easy access to Mrs. Selsby's room with his pass key; the evidence had been destroyed down in the boiler room, which was his domain; and his purchase of the new bungalow showed that he had an unexplained source of income.

But was Newth acting on his own or in league with someone else?

That question still remained to be investigated.

As did the matter of the fake stones in Lady Ridgleigh's jewellery. Had Newth done the same thing with them? Was he slowly working through the jewellery of all the lady residents of the Devereux? Would he in time turn his attention to all the beautiful stuff that the late Mr. Pargeter had so generously bestowed on his wife?

Not if Mrs. Pargeter had anything to do with it.

She decided she should consult another expert from the late Mr. Pargeter's address book.

"Hello. Byrom House Girls' School."

"Oh. Really? I wonder, would it be possible to speak to Mr. Melchett, please?"

"Just a moment. I'll see if the Bursar is in his office."

"Bursar?" murmured Mrs. Pargeter weakly. She was in the same public call box, and once again she had been referred to a number different from the one in the address book.

"Good morning." The voice was brisk and military, but still comfortingly recognisable.

"Fancy?"

"I beg your pardon?"

"Is that Fancy Melchett?"

"Major Melchett here. The Bursar. Are you a parent?"

"No."

"Oh." The voice became uncertain. "To whom am I speaking?"

"This is Melita Pargeter."

"Mrs. Pargeter! Good heavens!" All the reserve had gone, and the voice now flooded with warmth. "How wonderful to hear from you. I was really afraid that we'd lost touch, you know, after dear Mr. Pargeter . . ."

"Yes."

"Well, this is wonderful. Really cheered up my morning."

"What's with this 'Major' business?"

"Ah. Well, can't really have the Bursar of a girls' boarding school called 'Fancy,' can you?"

"Come to that, what's with all this 'Bursar' business?"

"Well, to be quite honest, I'd been thinking for some time of going str—" He stopped himself, thinking perhaps of listeners on the school switchboard, ". . . of, er, giving up the sort of work I had been doing, and when I saw this job advertised, it seemed to be just the ticket." His voice became more confidential. "Quite honestly, once Mr. Pargeter wasn't there, the fun seemed to have gone out of the other business. He really made it seem exciting. Oh, I continued for a bit, working with other people, but it just wasn't the same without him. . . ."

"No," Mrs. Pargeter agreed quietly.

"Anyway," the Bursar asked briskly, in his best "Major" voice, "what can I do for you?"

"Well, I'm not sure you can do anything. . . . I mean,

if you're completely out of that line of work nowadays."

"My dear lady, for you I'd do anything. Even go back to—" Once again he pulled himself up short, ". . . the sort of work we were discussing. Quite honestly, I owe so much to you and Mr. Pargeter, that you have only to say the word and I'll do whatever you require."

"I just want some information. . . ."

"About what?"

"Jewellery."

"Harrumph," said the Major. "I wonder, could you give me a number where I might call you back in about five minutes?"

She gave him the number of the call box and put the receiver down. Three minutes later the phone rang.

"So sorry about that. I'm calling from my house. Live on the premises, you know. This has the advantage of being a private line. Round a girls' school, you know, difficult to talk confidentially."

"That I can believe."

"But now we can talk about whatever we like. Jewellery, did you say?"

"Yes. I want to know who are the best fakers around."

"Fakers?" He sounded utterly bewildered.

"People who make imitation jewels."

"Oh. Sorry. Stupid. Thinking of Indian mystics. I'm a bloody idiot." He cleared his throat. "Right, with you now. You're setting up a substitution, are you?"

Mrs. Pargeter was very offended. "Fancy, you know I have never in my life been involved in anything criminal."

He was appropriately chastened. "No. Sorry. Of course. Don't know what I was thinking of. Forgive me."

"What I am doing is *investigating* a crime."

"Yes. Of course. Fully understand. Tell me, are we talking about bent or legit.?"

"Sorry?"

"Fakers. I mean, there are some who just do work for 'the business,' and others who do it quite publicly. You know, often happens when times get hard—people sell off the family jewels and have copies made. Thriving business—and, as I say, all above board."

"I think the name I'm after is probably legit., but I'd be grateful if you could give me some bent ones, too."

"No problem. It's a small field, anyway . . . for the ones who're any good. Only about four in the country who do decent work."

"Four legit. or four bent?"

"Four altogether. Of whom two are bent, one's legit., but doesn't ask questions, and one kicks with both feet."

"Hmm. What's the name of the legit. one who doesn't ask questions?"

"Desmond Chiddham. Very pukka. Workshop off Bond Street. Includes many of the crowned heads of Europe among his clientele. Indeed, when there's a Coronation or a Royal Wedding or that sort of number, people say you see more of his stuff than the genuine article."

"Ah. Well, could you give me his details, and the names and addresses of the other three?"

"Of course." Without a moment's hesitation, the Bursar reeled off the information.

"I'm most grateful to you, Fancy."

"Think nothing of it. Delighted to help. Do you know, just before he died, Mr. Pargeter took me on one side and asked if I'd look after you . . . if the occasion arose. You know, he really cared for you so much."

"Yes," said Mrs. Pargeter. "Yes, he did."

33

"I won't be in for lunch today, Miss Naismith."

"Oh? I believe I did mention, Mrs. Pargeter, that most residents tend to give such information to one of the staff."

"Yes. Yes, you did." Mrs. Pargeter smiled sweetly.

"Something interesting planned . . . ?" Miss Naismith fished.

"Oh yes," Mrs. Pargeter replied unhelpfully.

"Going far . . . ?"

"Quite a distance, yes."

"Ah."

"But I should be back for dinner."

"Oh. Good."

"Goodbye, then."

And Mrs. Pargeter left, treasuring the expression of frustrated curiosity on Miss Naismith's face.

The train from Littlehampton to London is not fast, but Mrs. Pargeter welcomed the time on her own to sit and think about the case (or the cases).

At Victoria she took a taxi to the Savoy Grill, where she had booked a table, and ate a substantial lunch. She remembered fondly how the late Mr. Pargeter had always been most insistent that she should have a good lunch.

From the Savoy she took another taxi to Desmond Chiddham's showroom and workshop off Bond Street. She had telephoned in the morning to make an appointment, but he was not free when she arrived. While she waited she looked at the displays of jewellery. It was all very good, and without the eye-glass she certainly couldn't have told whether the stones were real or not.

Desmond Chiddham was profuse with apologies for having kept her waiting. He was a small, bald man with rimless glasses and the upper-crust accent of someone who hasn't grown up with it but has mixed a lot with people who talk like that. Like his work, he was a fake.

"Well, Mrs. Pargeter, and what can I do for you?"

By way of answer, she produced her matching set of rubies from her handbag and laid them on his desk. The little eyes behind the glasses sparkled at the sight.

"I understand, Mr. Chiddham, that you could replace the jewels in these with artificial replicas."

"Oh, most certainly," he replied. "And replace them with stones that none but a trained eye would have the remotest suspicions about. And many trained eyes would have to look twice."

"Could you tell me how much that would cost?"

He named a price. It was high, but still represented

only ten per cent of the value of the stones he would be replacing.

"And, of course, Mrs. Pargeter, I am always happy to arrange the sale of the stones removed. Many of my clients like to take advantage of that part of the service. In that way, rather than their giving me money for the work, they end up by receiving money. Which is usually a more agreeable experience."

"Yes, I can see that. Could you tell me how long the work would take?"

"Well, our order book is always full, so it might be some time before we started, but once we were under way, it would take about ten days."

Not long enough for someone as vague as Mrs. Selsby to start worrying about having lost something.

Time to change gear and start getting more detailed information, Mrs. Pargeter thought. "I got in touch with you because I'd seen some excellent work you had done for someone else."

"Oh yes?" He looked gratified. "Might I ask who that person was?"

It was a risk, but one worth taking. "Lady Ridgleigh."

The risk paid off instantly. Desmond Chiddham gave a self-satisfied smile. "Oh yes, I've done a great deal of work for dear Lady Ridgleigh."

"Done most of the Ridgleigh family jewels, have you?"

"Ah, now . . ." He wagged a finger archly. "Must be discreet. Mustn't talk about my clients' affairs."

"Of course not." Mrs. Pargeter paused. "One piece you'd done for Lady Ridgleigh that I particularly liked was an opal necklace. . . ."

"I remember it well. Particularly difficult to achieve, an imitation of an opal," he said in a tone of self-congratulation.

"And a beautiful matching emerald set . . ."

"Yes, remember that, too. Mind you, you're talking some years back. My relationship with Lady Ridgleigh," he added smugly, "is of long standing."

"Of course. She also showed me a matching sapphire set . . ."

"Remember doing that."

". . . and some turquoise ear-rings."

"Yes. We're talking more recently now, of course."

Mrs. Pargeter did not allow her inward elation to show. The last two items she had mentioned did not belong to Lady Ridgleigh; they had belonged to the late Mrs. Selsby.

"So you see a lot of Lady Ridgleigh, do you?"

He looked a trifle piqued. This direct question meant he must qualify his name-dropping and define the extent of his hobnobbing with the aristocracy. "Well, I don't actually see her that often. Our dealings are conducted through an intermediary."

"Oh?"

"One of her staff tends to come up with the latest item for me to work on. I suppose he's a butler or footman. . . ."

"What's his name?" asked Mrs. Pargeter ingenuously.

"Unusual name," replied Desmond Chiddham. "Newth."

34

Mrs. Pargeter was back at the Devereux just after Newth had changed into his red jacket and opened the Schooner Bar. He had served Miss Naismith her first "Perrier," which had disappeared with its customary despatch before the residents came in. He had given Eulalie Vance a white wine and soda, and was just going through the routine of asking Colonel Wicksteed and Mr. Dawlish what they wanted to drink, when Mrs. Pargeter entered.

"Pleasant day, I trust?" asked Miss Naismith, by now nursing a glass of real Perrier.

"Yes, thank you," said Mrs. Pargeter charmingly, but uninformatively.

After suitable deliberation, Colonel Wicksteed decided that he would have "a large Famous Grouse" and

Mr. Dawlish "a small dry sherry." Newth then turned to Mrs. Pargeter.

"I think I'll have a change this week, Kevin, love."

A shadow of pain crossed Miss Naismith's face.

"Yes, give me a large gin and tonic. Start out in a different way, and maybe things'll turn out different, eh?"

"Sorry? I'm not with you."

"What I mean, Colonel, is that we don't want another week like the last one, do we?"

"Oh, I see what you mean."

"We had enough excitements then to last a lifetime, didn't we?"

"Still, we don't want to dwell on the past," Miss Naismith smoothly interposed, as ever endeavouring to scoop up the conversation before it dropped to an unsuitably low level.

But Mrs. Pargeter was not to be deflected. For reasons of her own, she wanted the crimes of the previous week discussed. "I don't know . . . two deaths and a robbery."

Miss Naismith winced visibly. "I think it has always been true that the best approach to any misfortune is to put it from one's mind and look ahead to the future."

"Oh yes," the Colonel agreed, adding one of his customary misquotations to reinforce the point. " 'If you can look at Triumph and Disaster, and treat those two old frauds the same way,' what?"

"Exactly," said Miss Naismith, as if in some obscure way this confirmed what she had said.

"I don't know, though," Mrs. Pargeter persisted. "I mean, we can't pretend that those things didn't happen. Nor can we pretend they haven't set us all thinking, human nature being what it is."

"The fact that human nature is what it is," observed

Miss Naismith, "has never seemed to me to be a cause for celebration."

"What, you mean we should pretend we're not all inquisitive old busybodies who're dying to know everything about everyone?"

"I think such an approach to life would be preferable, yes."

"Oh, come on, Miss Naismith, admit it, you're as nosey as the rest of us."

The joshing approach, as Mrs. Pargeter had anticipated, did not go down well with Miss Naismith, who turned her personal thermostat down a good ten degrees.

"Curiosity, as you say, may be a human instinct, Mrs. Pargeter, but it is one that should ideally be curbed at an early age by a proper education."

"That's a point of view," Mrs. Pargeter agreed blithely. She was enjoying herself. After the accusation about the theft of Mrs. Selsby's jewels, she knew that the balance of power between them had shifted, and that she could press quite hard to antagonise Miss Naismith without harmful effects. She wanted the murders and the theft discussed to see if they prompted any unexpected reactions; so, braving the deterrence in the proprietress's eye, she pressed on.

"But it is interesting, isn't it? I mean, as I say, two deaths and a robbery—it's the stuff of detective stories."

This caught Mr. Dawlish's imagination. "By George, yes! Back to Holmes and Watson, eh, Wicksteed?"

"Yes. Do you see yourself as a sleuth, old man? Tracking down the murderer to his lair, what?"

Mr. Dawlish giggled with delight. "Maybe that's my *métier*. Maybe I have spent my entire life being unsuccessful at other things, because all the time I was cut out to be a detective, eh?"

Mrs. Pargeter encouraged him gently. "Maybe so. And, if that were the case, what would your thinking be about this case?"

"Oh, Good Lord. Haven't a thought in my head."

"Colonel?"

"No idea. Not my speed, this kind of thing, I'm afraid."

"Eulalie . . . ?"

"What? Sorry?" The actress looked up from her drink, as if she had been dragged back from the depths of fantasy. "No. No. I hadn't given it any thought."

"Kevin?"

"I haven't given the matter any consideration either, I'm afraid, Madam," the barman replied primly.

Miss Naismith sighed with relief. "Well, that seems to have exhausted this particular—"

"The only thing that struck me about it," Mrs. Pargeter went on firmly, "is that, if this were a detective story, you could guarantee that the three cases would be connected."

"What three cases?" asked Eulalie.

"The two deaths and the robbery."

Mr. Dawlish looked puzzled. "What have the two deaths got to do with it?"

"Well, if this were a detective story, you could safely assume that the two deaths were murders."

There was an awkward silence, which Miss Naismith finally thought proper to break. "I'm afraid I cannot regard that suggestion as being in the best of taste."

"I wasn't suggesting it seriously. Only saying that, if this *were* a detective story, that would be a safe assumption to make."

"Well, this *isn't* a detective story." Miss Naismith placed her empty glass on the counter. "I may say, I was always brought up to believe that detective stories are the products of trivial minds—and the entertainment of equally trivial ones." She turned towards the door. "I believe it is nearly time for dinner."

After she had left the room, the others downed their drinks rather hastily, regretting the slight "atmosphere" that had been created. "Atmospheres" were avoided at the Devereux.

But Mrs. Pargeter was unrepentant. She had set up the scene deliberately to check out certain reactions and, though she could not claim to have observed anything startling, she did not feel that the exercise had been wasted.

It was part of a new approach to the case. Hitherto she had been discreet and unobtrusive. Now she was beginning to think she might have to assert herself a little more, show a higher profile, maybe even use shock tactics to get nearer the solution to the mystery.

Newth was picking up glasses from the counter. The other residents had gone through to the Admiral's Dining Room.

"Oh, Kevin," Mrs. Pargeter said casually, "I went up to London today."

"Really, Madam? I hope that was enjoyable." The prim formality remained in his voice.

"Yes. I went to see someone near Bond Street."

"Oh?"

"A specialist in imitation jewellery called Desmond Chiddham."

Having decided to use shock tactics, she couldn't have asked for more satisfactory shock reactions. The colour drained from Newth's face. One hand reached up to press against his chest, while the other went forward to support him against the bar. Mrs. Pargeter wondered whether he was about to collapse again as he had outside the bungalow in Lancing. Once again she was made aware of what a very sick man he was.

But he didn't collapse. Not quite. He just swayed, looking at her speechlessly.

"I wonder . . . maybe you and I could have a talk? With Lady Ridgleigh, too, I think that would perhaps be best. . . ."

His tongue licked across dry lips, but still no words came.

"What, in the Seaview Lounge, about half-past eight . . . do you think that would suit . . . ?"

Newth nodded, and Mrs. Pargeter went through to enjoy her dinner in the Admiral's Dining Room.

35

MONDAY

11 MARCH—8:15 p.m.—*As I anticipated, it looks very much as if two murders will not have been enough. Mrs. Mendlingham died because she could have incriminated me about Mrs. Selsby's murder, and now I fear that there is someone else who may have information that could restrict my freedom.*

I have been suspicious of her since she arrived. There is about her a watchfulness, which I am beginning to find unnerving. She misses nothing, and I suspect she has the intelligence to make connections between the pieces of information she picks up.

I've a nasty feeling that she's on to me. At first I thought she was just nosey, poking around the hotel because she's curious by nature. But now I'm coming to the conclusion that her inquisitiveness is not random. She is behaving almost like a professional investigator.

For a start, she appears to possess a professional's equipment—and the expertise to go with it. When I saw her in the small hours of Monday morning, I'm fairly sure that she had just broken into the Office. I can only assume that she used some sort of skeleton key. That sounds uncomfortably professional to me.

Then tonight in the bar she said something that suggested that she's definitely on to me. That business about the crimes being linked came too close to the truth for comfort.

I don't know how much she knows yet, but she's getting there, and I can't take the risk of giving her much more time. So far as I know, she hasn't said anything to the police yet, and I must see to it that she doesn't get the chance.

Yes, what I'm saying is that there has to be a third murder. I would like to have more leisure to plan, to ensure that this one looks as accidental as the others, but I think this time it's too urgent.

She has to go—and quickly!

36

Mrs. Pargeter lay on her bed for a little while after dinner. She was tired after the exertions of the day, following on the sequence of interrupted nights. She couldn't take it like she used to. Though very fit for her age, there was no way round the fact that she had reached sixty-seven. And she was going to need all her strength for the interview ahead of her.

She must have dozed off, and woke with a start, afraid that she might have missed her rendezvous. But no, her watch told her she had only been asleep for ten minutes.

As often happens after a brief nap, her mouth tasted foul. She went to the basin and cleaned her teeth, but still the rusty taste lingered.

"Make sure you always have sweet breath." That had

been another of the late Mr. Pargeter's pieces of advice. "There is no excuse for smelly breath. It's one of those things that is quite controllable."

For this reason, although her own breath was usually sweet, it was Mrs. Pargeter's habit to have an atomiser spray around in her bedroom (or in her handbag if she was going out). She had always taken to heart any advice that the late Mr. Pargeter had given her (and she knew how particularly important it was for older people to be careful about their breath).

She reached to her bedside table now for the atomiser and directed a couple of sharp puffs into her mouth. The taste of the spray made her feel immediately better.

She put the atomiser down on her bedside table and checked her face and hair in the mirror. Then she picked up her handbag and went straight down to the Seaview Lounge.

Lady Ridgleigh and Newth were already installed in the armchairs in the bay when she entered the room. The curtains had not been drawn, only one small lamp was on on the far wall, and from the sea a faint, greyish light glowed, outlining the two figures against the windows.

Mrs. Pargeter drew up a small stool and positioned herself between the two armchairs. She was very aware of the ponderous ticking of the grandfather clock.

"Thank you for coming," she said softly.

The bony outline of Lady Ridgleigh's head was graciously inclined.

There was a silence.

Then Newth cleared his throat. "I have told her Ladyship what you told me—that you've been to see Mr. Chiddham."

"May I ask," Lady Ridgleigh drawled, "why you did

that? Perhaps it will explain why I've been summoned here in this rather melodramatic manner."

"I was interested in what had happened to Mrs. Selsby's jewels. And what had happened to your jewels before that."

"Ah." Any hope there might have been in Lady Ridgleigh's voice had gone from that monosyllable. "So now I assume you know what happened to them?"

"I think so."

"Tell me, then. I'll let you know whether your speculation is correct or not." Lady Ridgleigh sounded reproving; there was in her voice the tone that the Queen might be expected to use to a Commonwealth leader who has just announced his intention of leaving the Commonwealth.

"Well, the way I see it is this. . . ." Mrs. Pargeter began comfortably. "After your husband's death, you found that you were very financially embarrassed. You told me once that he had lost all your money, but I still think you were shocked by quite how much he had lost.

"Still, a lot of widows have found themselves in that position, and what most of them have to do is just swallow their pride and settle down to managing on a smaller income . . . effectively they have to cut their standard of living. To do that was very hard for you. You'd always had large houses, servants. . . . To admit you could no longer maintain that style of life was a bitter pill for you to swallow."

"Yes, but I did it," said Lady Ridgleigh with some asperity. "Do you think, when I was a young gel, I expected to end my life somewhere like the Devereux Hotel?"

Mrs. Pargeter would have liked Miss Naismith to hear the contempt that was put into those last two words.

Gentility was one thing, but aristocracy something else. To Lady Ridgleigh, living at the Devereux was definitely slumming.

"Yes, all right, you cut down your standard of living. You sold the house, houses maybe."

"Not worth anything, though. Froggie had mortgaged them all to the hilt." There was still a hint of pride when she spoke of her late husband's improvidence.

"Yes, you remained hard up. Even living here. And then of course you had . . . other expenses."

There was a long silence. Mrs. Pargeter could sense the intensity with which Newth was looking at her. It was a disorienting, uncomfortable feeling.

"What do you mean by 'other expenses'?" Lady Ridgleigh asked finally.

"I mean your son."

"What do you know about Miles? You've hardly met him."

"I don't know a great deal. Just that he takes after his father where money's concerned."

"So? What's wrong with that? God, I wouldn't want to spawn some penny-pinching little wage-slave. Miles knows his place in society and he enjoys himself. If you can't have a good time when you're young, what's the point of life?"

"Miles is thirty-six," said Mrs. Pargeter softly.

"What do you mean by that?"

"Just that he's a bit old to be behaving like a deb's delight. Isn't it about time he got a job?"

"He hasn't found anything suitable," Lady Ridgleigh replied, dismissing the subject.

"Well, I would think he's a bit old still to be sponging on his mother. . . ."

Lady Ridgleigh flared up. "How dare you use that word in connection with my son! What business is it of yours how he behaves? And what business of yours is it if I choose to . . . help him a little with his expenses?"

"Not my business at all."

"Exactly. Thank you. I happen to believe that someone of his age shouldn't have to worry about money. In fact, I don't think anyone should have to. Worrying about money is demeaning, depressing, and unutterably vulgar!"

"I agree. The fact remains that a large percentage of the population spend most of their time worrying about it."

"Which is exactly why I have always been determined that Miles shouldn't."

"Even if it means committing criminal acts to keep him in funds?"

"Criminal acts? What on earth are you talking about?"

"We're back to Desmond Chiddham."

"I don't know Mr. Chiddham personally. I have done business with him, but I'm afraid if he is a criminal, I can hardly see that it's my responsibility."

"No. How did you hear about his service?"

"Through a friend," came the huffy reply. "A friend, who had experienced similar embarrassments, recommended him."

"And the idea was that you should send him the Ridgleigh family jewels, he should replace the stones with replicas, sell the original stones for you and pay you the profit?"

"That, I believe, was the arrangement."

"You didn't ask him to remake any of the settings in cheaper metals?"

"Good heavens, no. The idea was that the jewellery should look as much as possible as it had before."

"But it didn't, did it?"

"What do you mean?"

"It didn't look good enough to meet with your high standards, did it? Which is why you never wore it once it had been altered . . . why you continued to wear your one remaining genuine necklace, your pearls, all the time . . . even with clothes for which they were inappropriate."

"Yes. Very well. That's true."

"But the jewels were good enough to maintain your image of wealth with someone like Miss Naismith. Which is why, although they are virtually worthless, you still keep them in the safe in the Office."

"That may be true, but I don't see how it's relevant." Lady Ridgleigh was at her haughtiest. "And I would now like you to substantiate your accusations that I have been guilty of criminal acts."

"First, I want you to tell me how Newth came to be involved in your dealings with Desmond Chiddham."

"I could hardly be expected to handle the transactions myself, could I?" She spoke as if this idea were totally incongruous. "Obviously, when I was living in the big house, I would have had a member of staff to do that sort of thing for me. Here . . . well, there was no one else, so I asked Newth if he would help me, and he was good enough to oblige."

"And what was the deal with him?"

"I'm sorry. I'm afraid I don't understand that expression."

"Presumably you wanted discretion. How much did you pay Newth for his silence?"

Lady Ridgleigh's reply was tinged with distaste at the idea of speaking so nakedly of money. "Newth was paid a ten-per-cent handling fee."

"Right," said Mrs. Pargeter. "So what happened when the jewellery ran out?"

"I don't understand what you mean."

"When you had sold off all the stones from all the valuable pieces you possessed, what did you do?"

The bony shoulders shrugged in the half-light. "Well, what could I do? I sold a few shares. I tried to cut down on my expenses—gave up drinking alcohol and so on. And I kept putting off the moment when I would have to sell the pearls. But I feared that moment had finally come—until this week."

"This week?"

"The happy news of Mrs. Selsby's bequests to all of the people living here at the Devereux."

"Oh yes. Of course. A very welcome lifeline."

"Indeed."

"So . . . since her name's come up—what about Mrs. Selsby's jewels?"

Lady Ridgleigh looked blank. "Well, they were stolen, weren't they? I don't think Mrs. Selsby's jewels have anything to do with me."

"No, I don't think they have," said Mrs. Pargeter slowly, and turned in her chair to face Newth.

He was no longer looking at her with that disturbing intensity. His eyes were now focused on the highly polished toe-caps of his shoes.

"So that was all off your own bat, was it, Kevin?"

"I don't know what you mean," he mumbled.

"Oh, I think you do. It was a good idea. Lady Ridgleigh had shown you how it could be done. You'd taken enough of her jewellery to Desmond Chiddham. But you were only on ten per cent there, weren't you? And, besides, the supply was running out.

"Then you thought of Mrs. Selsby. Dear, dozy, half-blind Mrs. Selsby. She had a lot of jewellery lying around. She wouldn't notice if a piece went missing for a week or two, would she? And her eyesight certainly wasn't good enough to detect that the stones had been replaced. What's more, with her stuff, you were taking a hundred per cent of the profit. And, to make even more, why not have the settings replaced too?"

"You're talking rubbish," said Newth. But he didn't sound as if he was even convincing himself.

"No, I'm not. You'd got yourself a very good little business sorted out there. Very profitable. Easily make enough to buy a nice retirement bungalow in Lancing."

Newth's head shot up at this.

"Yes, I know, Kevin. I know all about it. Your little scheme was absolutely foolproof, wasn't it? Or rather it was foolproof as long as no one found out. But if anyone did find out, then they could cause trouble for you, couldn't they?"

Newth had half-risen in his seat, and was looking at Mrs. Pargeter with an expression of fixed hatred.

"How did Mrs. Selsby find out what was going on, Kevin?" she asked softly.

He was now on his feet, towering over her, every muscle of his body bristling with threat.

"I'll get you!" he hissed through his teeth. "I'll get you for this!" For a moment he was about to strike her, but he seemed to change his mind, and backed towards the door.

"Nobody's going to catch me," he muttered. "Nobody's going to catch me!"

He opened the door and rushed out.

Mrs. Pargeter hurried into the Entrance Hall, and was just in time to see the front doors bang behind him. She went outside and saw his figure running madly along the sea front away from the Devereux. He was too far away for her to contemplate giving chase.

She felt completely drained as she went back into the

hotel. Wearily she dragged herself up the stairs to her bedroom.

Meanwhile, in the Seaview Lounge, Lady Ridgleigh stayed in her armchair and called out peevishly to the empty room, "I wish someone would tell me what the devil's going on."

37

Mrs. Pargeter flopped onto her bed. She felt trembly, in need of some sort of restorative. For a moment she contemplated the effort of going back down to the Schooner Bar for a brandy. Then, wryly, she remembered that there was no one at the moment around to man the Schooner Bar.

She wondered where Newth would go. She didn't think he'd get far.

Soon, she knew, she'd have to call the police. Soon she'd have to explain the reasons why she had reached the conclusion that Newth was a murderer.

But it'd keep for a little while. She was going to need all her wits about her for that conversation. Just give herself a few minutes for recuperation.

She knew why she felt so exhausted. It was the

release of tension. She had been really terrified of Newth, because she could recognise the logic of a murderer's mind. The person who had killed Mrs. Selsby had also killed Mrs. Mendlingham when she revealed that she had witnessed the first murder. Mrs. Pargeter, by her hints in the Schooner Bar that evening, had alerted the murderer to her own suspicions, and from that moment had put herself at the top of the list of prospective victims.

It was a huge relief to have survived that interview with Newth.

She felt drowsy, as if she might drift off to sleep.

But still there was a nasty metallic taste in her mouth. Probably just dry, she thought, another reflection of the strain I've just been under for the last hour.

Still, she didn't want to wake again with a nasty taste. She reached sleepily round for the atomiser on her bedside table and brought it to her mouth.

It was an uneven ridge she felt along the side of the little cylinder that stopped her short.

She peered at the tiny atomiser and saw that the two parts of it were marginally out of alignment.

She was instantly alert. The unit was sealed, but with a little force could be opened. She tried it. The cylinder unscrewed without any force at all. It had been opened before.

With unpleasant foreboding, she continued to unscrew the top from the atomiser and lowered her nose to sniff the exposed liquid within.

She recognised the smell instantly. Though the late Mr. Pargeter had never used toxic substances in his own business, he had occasionally been at risk from other less scrupulous operators in the same field; and among the many other useful things he had taught his wife had been how to recognise the major poisons.

The atomiser contained cyanide.

Mrs. Pargeter went rigid with shock.

Not just shock because someone had tried to kill her.

But shock because she'd used the atomiser without adverse effects immediately before going down to the Seaview Lounge, where she had found Newth.

Which meant that Newth could not have had the opportunity to fill it with cyanide.

Which meant that the murderer at the Devereux was somebody else.

38

12 MARCH—7:30 a.m.—*Damn! It didn't work. For the first time one of my little shots has failed to reach its target. I suppose it always was the least likely to work. With the other murders there was never any question about the method's efficacy, because I was there to do it myself. This was my first attempt at a remote control murder, and I suppose for that reason the most susceptible to failure.*

I know it didn't work, because I have just seen my intended victim walking down to breakfast. All right, I suppose it's possible that she hasn't used the spray yet and my scheme still has a chance of success, but instinct tells me that is not the case. What is much more likely, I fear, is that not only has the cyanide in the spray failed, it has also alerted her to my intentions towards her.

I must tread warily. And I must watch her like a hawk. Any attempt she makes to contact the police must be thwarted. Indeed, nothing has changed. Now more than ever I have to murder her. But the next time there must be no mistakes. No more overconfident remote control ideas. The next time I must get her alone and do it in person, so that I can be sure that she's dead.

In the meantime, I will act naturally. Down to breakfast with me. Even after this recent setback, I still feel good. Who would ever have imagined that I would derive such pleasure from leading a double life!

39

Mrs. Pargeter sat over her kipper and looked round at the other residents breakfasting in the Admiral's Dining Room. It was a peaceful scene of geriatric gentility, marred only by her knowledge that one of the other people in the room was a murderer.

She looked at them one by one.

Lady Ridgleigh was spearing small pieces of bacon with her fork and stabbing them into her mouth. She had avoided Mrs. Pargeter's eye that morning, mindful of their conversation of the night before. But that conversation had ruled her out as a candidate for the title of the Devereux murderer.

Miss Wardstone munched disapprovingly on her dry toast and marmalade. Butter, being something she might enjoy, was rigorously excluded from her diet, and, from the expression on her face, she had selected the tartest of marmalades. Miss Wardstone exuded such unadulterated bitterness that it was tempting to think some might have been channelled into murder. She had made no secret of her delight at Mrs. Selsby's death and her impatience to claim the old lady's sea-front room.

But, reluctantly, Mrs. Pargeter had to rule this candidate out too.

It was the cyanide attack that put Miss Wardstone out of the running. Mrs. Pargeter felt convinced that the attempt on her life had been prompted by what she had said in the Schooner Bar the night before. Though she hadn't intended it quite that way, she now realised that her words could have been interpreted by the murderer as a warning that she was on his or her track. And, of course, because of Miss Wardstone's avoidance of anything that might dilute her natural sourness, she had not been in the bar the previous night.

That left three—the two gentlemen, already deep in their customary conversation of gnomic non sequiturs, and Eulalie Vance.

Mrs. Pargeter thought about the former actress. There was certainly a lot of emotion there on the surface, but that might hide more complex emotions surging underneath. The heart that is worn on the sleeve is not always the true heart. And an actress is trained to deception. Mrs. Pargeter wondered what possible motive Eulalie could have had against Mrs. Selsby.

"Mrs. Pargeter."

The voice was so close that she started. Absorbed in her thoughts, she had not noticed anyone else come into the room.

"Good morning, Miss Naismith."

"I wonder," said the proprietress silkily, "whether it

190

would be possible for you to step into the Office for a quiet word in a moment . . . ?"

"Yes. Of course. Time for me just to have another cup of tea?"

"Certainly, Mrs. Pargeter."

As Miss Naismith glided out of the Admiral's Dining Room, it occurred to Mrs. Pargeter that there was another person who had witnessed what she had said the previous night in the Schooner Bar.

"Come in," called the voice from inside the Office door.

Mrs. Pargeter entered. Miss Naismith sat behind her desk, looking atypically ill at ease. Her fingers fiddled nervously with what appeared to be a paper-knife.

"Mrs. Pargeter. Thank you for coming. Please sit down."

Mrs. Pargeter obeyed. Miss Naismith's fingers still fiddled, twitchily feeling along the blade of the knife. This was out of character, a lapse of breeding that denoted considerable inward perturbation.

"What's the problem, then?" asked Mrs. Pargeter comfortably.

"The fact is . . ." Miss Naismith rose from her desk and moved across to check that the door was closed. "The fact is that something rather distressing has occurred."

"Oh yes?"

"Yes."

Miss Naismith's voice was now behind her, but Mrs. Pargeter did not turn round as she asked, "What's that, then?"

There was a long silence, as though the proprietress were steeling herself to some distasteful duty.

At last the words came out, expelled by a ferocious

effort of will. "The fact is, Mrs. Pargeter, that I owe you an apology."

After this painful sentence had been spoken, Miss Naismith seemed to relax. She moved back to her desk, sat down and placed the paper-knife on its surface, neatly aligned with her blotter.

"You may remember, Mrs. Pargeter, that we had an unfortunate misunderstanding a few days ago."

"Oh?" Mrs. Pargeter wasn't going to make it easy; she was determined that Miss Naismith should finish up every scrap of her humble pie and then wipe the plate.

"With regard to Mrs. Selsby's jewels . . . "

"Ah."

"And I made an accusation that was, in retrospect, extremely ill-considered."

Mrs. Pargeter smiled pleasantly.

"The fact is, I have now discovered who the real perpetrator of the crime was."

Mrs. Pargeter didn't volunteer that she also knew. Apart from anything else, she wanted to know how Miss Naismith had found out the truth.

"The identity of the criminal is not, I'm afraid, something that reflects favourably on the Devereux."

Mrs. Pargeter bit back the temptation to say, "You amaze me."

"Mrs. Selsby's jewels were stolen by a member of my staff." Oh, how it hurt her to say the words!

Mrs. Pargeter allowed herself the indulgence of a raised eyebrow.

"Newth, Mrs. Pargeter. It was Newth. I am terribly disappointed to have to say this, and I feel utterly betrayed, but I'm afraid it is the truth."

Mrs. Pargeter still kept silence, confident that all the details would come out if she bided her time.

"Perhaps because of a guilty conscience or perhaps because he thought that his crimes were about to be discovered, it seems that Newth ran away from the hotel last night. Unfortunately, however, he is not a fit man—he has been suffering for some years from a heart condition—and the effort of running . . . or the strains of his guilt . . . led him to have a heart attack. He collapsed, it seems, on the outskirts of Littlehampton, where he was discovered in the small hours of this morning and taken to hospital.

"There he was examined and found to be in need of major surgery—open-heart surgery, I believe they call it. When he heard this, it seems that, aware of the risks of such an operation, he wanted to make a clean breast of his crimes. The police were summoned to the hospital, where Newth confessed that not only did he steal Mrs. Selsby's jewellery the night after she died, but also that he had stolen it before!"

Mrs. Pargeter nodded, and Miss Naismith looked rather disappointed. She had expected more reaction to this bombshell.

"Apparently—and you can imagine how distressed I was to hear this—over a period of months Newth had been stealing individual items of Mrs. Selsby's jewellery and replacing them with imitations!"

This revelation was rewarded by no more than another nod.

Miss Naismith looked disgruntled, but had to continue. "I need not tell you how shocked I was by this revelation. The police telephoned me about half an hour ago and I could hardly believe what they told me. However, I am reluctantly forced to the conclusion that it is the truth."

There was another silence. Miss Naismith was being made to work every inch of the way.

"So, Mrs. Pargeter, once again I apologise. I cannot tell you how appalled I am by what has happened. I have spent a good part of my life building up the reputation of the Devereux, and to have that reputation sullied by a crime on the premises is a severe blow to everything that I have ever believed in."

Yes, Mrs. Pargeter thought, you really mean that. The gentility, the "niceness," the "class," of the Devereux matters to you more than anything in the world. Which is why you would never threaten its image by committing a crime here yourself. Which is why I must strike you too off my list of murder suspects.

"So, Mrs. Pargeter . . . Please. Please may I ask you to accept my apology . . . ?"

Mrs. Pargeter was not vindictive. She had had her triumph, she had won the battle, and was not the sort to gloat over her victory.

"Of course, love," she said, and held out her hand.

Miss Naismith reached hers daintily across the table and they shook hands.

Not soul-mates, perhaps, but at least no longer in a state of open war.

40

Eulalie Vance was sitting alone in the Seaview Lounge when Mrs. Pargeter entered after her interview with Miss Naismith. The former actress was ensconced in one of the armchairs that were usually occupied by Colonel Wicksteed and Mr. Dawlish. She was looking out over the mournful sea.

In her hands she held a hard-covered dark blue diary.

"Good morning," said Mrs. Pargeter companionably, settling into the other armchair.

"Good morning," Eulalie contrived to make the words a long sigh as well as a greeting.

"You don't look too perky."

"No."

"Problems?"

This was met by a little laugh that seemed to suggest

that a new word was needed to describe the sort of problems Eulalie had.

"Anything that talking would help?" asked Mrs. Pargeter. "I mean, I don't want to pry, but . . . you know, a trouble shared and all that . . . "

"Yes." Very quickly the actress made the decision that talking would help. "Are you a creature of passion, Melita?"

"I *have* been," Mrs. Pargeter replied cautiously.

"Then you know what it is like to have done things in a moment of passion, things that you subsequently come to regret?"

"Ye-es."

"I have always been a slave to my passions," Eulalie Vance announced with a kind of helpless pride. "As a result, there are many things in my life that I have come to regret."

"And some, presumably, that you remember fondly?"

"Of course. God, at my age what have I got left but memories? No, there have been moments . . . moments again of passion, but of a different kind, that I will treasure till my dying day. Which," she added gloomily, "may, I fear, not be far away."

"Oh, come on. You're good for a few years yet."

This idea raised a desperate little laugh of cynicism. Then Eulalie's eyes narrowed and she looked hard at her companion. "Do you believe that all is fair in love and war?"

Mrs. Pargeter maintained her cautious approach. "I've certainly heard it *said*."

"*Amor vincit omnia*," Eulalie announced despairingly.

"I've heard *that* said, too."

"Yes. What I mean is that love is so powerful, love so

upturns the soul, that anything can be done in the cause of love."

"You mean that someone in love is above the restrictions of conventional morality?"

"Exactly!" To emphasise her point, Eulalie banged the diary down on her knee. Then she became quiet and abstracted, as if the director had told her that the next scene was to show a marked change of mood. "I believe . . . firmly believe . . . that love can justify anything. But when someone is dead, it is hard not to feel the prickings of conscience. . . ."

"When a lover's dead . . . ?" Mrs. Pargeter prompted gently.

"Huh." Another wild little cry of despair. "Nearly all my lovers, I fear, are dead. That is perhaps the ultimate cruelty of age, for those of us who believe in reality."

"What do you mean exactly?"

"I mean there are two sorts of people. There are those who separate love and life, who compromise, settle down with one person, marry perhaps, and keep love as a cherished fantasy. And then there are those who live the fantasy, those who do not dream of one perfect lover, but take the lover of the moment—and take all the heartbreak that involves. . . ."

"Ye-es." Mrs. Pargeter thought she should qualify this generalisation. After all, it didn't match her own experience. "There are of course some who combine both, who find their fantasies are matched by reality."

Eulalie dismissed the existence of such earthbound souls with a toss of her coiled hair. "The disadvantage is, for those who have lived the reality, as their lovers die, they too are left to feed on fantasy."

"Yes, I suppose they are." Mrs. Pargeter wasn't sure

where all this was leading. "What exactly do you mean? Has one of your lovers died recently?"

"Not one of my lovers, no."

"Who, then?"

"The wife of one of my lovers," Eulalie Vance said on one sustained, soft breath.

"So does that mean your lover is now free for you?"

"Oh no." She elongated the "no" to almost impossible dimensions. "He, I fear, is long dead. No, that is the irony. While we were together, how we longed for his wife's death. 'If it weren't for my wife . . .' he would always say. If it hadn't been for his wife, we could have been together years ago. But no. She lived on, and he felt a duty to her. In spite of the passion he and I shared, he still felt a duty to his wife. And, in time, he went back to her."

"Ah. Well . . . That happens quite often, I believe."

"Oh yes. It's a cliché. To think that the love between me and Norton Selsby should have been reduced to a cliché!"

"Selsby?" said Mrs. Pargeter.

"Yes."

"Like . . . Mrs. Selsby?"

"Yes." There was now a wildness in Eulalie Vance's eyes. "Mrs. Selsby. That's the final bitter irony, isn't it? I end up by chance living in the same hotel with the faded, pale nonentity to whom duty made my lover return."

"It must have been difficult for you," Mrs. Pargeter said judiciously. "Was anything said?"

"What could be said? She never knew."

"Never knew her husband had had an affair with you?"

"No. Never suspected a thing. For six months Norton and I lived the heady perfection of love, drained the cup of passion to its dregs . . . and his bloodless wife continued her tedious domestic round and didn't notice a thing."

"In some ways that was rather fortunate, wasn't it? I mean, if she *had* known, it could have made your both living here rather awkward, couldn't it?"

"Huh. Oh no, it wasn't difficult for her. Nothing had ever been difficult for her. In spite of her coldness, Norton gave her everything, bowed to her every whim. But . . ." Some director had once taught Eulalie the effectiveness of a mid-sentence pause, ". . . how do you think it must have been for *me*?"

"It can't have been easy. I can see that," Mrs. Pargeter conceded.

"Not easy? You have a gift for understatement. To be constantly reminded of the past, to have constantly before me the pale, insipid thing for which he gave me up . . . you cannot conceive the torment."

"So what did you do about it?"

"I was very good. Dear God, how good I was! I did nothing. I said nothing. I suppressed all the emotions boiling within my breast." She clasped the diary to the Indian print of her substantial bosom. "I tortured myself, but I could stand it. I could stand it . . . until a couple of weeks ago. . . ."

"What happened a couple of weeks ago?" asked Mrs. Pargeter quietly.

"For some reason the conversation got around to letters . . . old letters, rereading old letters. Lady Ridgleigh, I think, started it. She said how she had kept every word that Froggie—that was her husband—had ever sent her. And then Mrs. Selsby said she had kept all Norton's letters."

"And you were worried that there were some from you?"

"Good heavens, no! There were no letters between us. I wanted to write, but Norton said no. He was always worried about the risk of being found out, so he never wrote to me, and he wouldn't let me write to him."

"So what was your problem when Mrs. Selsby mentioned the letters?"

Eulalie Vance looked amazed at this lack of comprehension. "Well, the fact that they existed! There was I, having experienced the greatest love there ever was, and I had nothing to cherish but my memories. And there was she, with a whole set of mementoes of her own anaemic, loveless relationship with the same man."

"Did she imply that what she had were love letters?"

"Yes." Eulalie Vance laughed harshly. "Which only goes to make it more ridiculous."

Mrs. Pargeter thought she was beginning to see the picture. Norton Selsby had probably had a perfectly satisfactory physical relationship with his wife. Eulalie had been his "bit on the side." After six months, suffering partly from boredom and partly from risk-fatigue, he had, like so many men before him, decided to quit while he was ahead. So he had "gone back to his wife," who had welcomed him without elaborate ceremony, never having realised he'd been away.

But, though she could easily sketch in the likely scenario of the affair, it was harder to guess at its more recent consequences.

"What happened?" she asked.

"Happened?"

"When you found out about the letters?"

"Well, I . . . As I said, I am a slave to passion, a creature of impulse. I did something impulsive. It was also . . . cruel."

"And that was the thing you were saying you regretted?"

Eulalie Vance nodded, her face set in a tragic mask. "It was just vindictive. At the time I thought it would make me feel better, I thought the shock of what I did would clear the emotions inside me. But now that she's dead . . ."

"You feel sorry you did it?"

Eulalie nodded again.

"Tell me exactly what happened."

It was as if the director had told her that this narration would be most effective delivered numbly, quietly, without overt emotion.

"It was about three days before she died . . . just before you came to the hotel. I went into her room when I knew everyone would be downstairs waiting for tea. She didn't keep anything locked up. It was easy to find what I was looking for."

"The letters . . . ?"

"Yes. They were in one of the drawers of her bureau, a thick bunch, tied with a pink ribbon—or perhaps it had been a red ribbon and faded, I don't know. I knew they were the right ones. Even though Norton never wrote me letters, I knew his handwriting. I took them."

"And what did you find out when you read them?"

"I didn't read them. I couldn't bring myself to read them. No, I'm afraid I did something wicked."

"Yes . . . ?"

"I took them down to the basement and I threw them on the boiler. I destroyed them."

Mrs. Pargeter left a pause, of which Eulalie's director would surely have approved, before asking, " And did Mrs. Selsby say anything to you about the loss of her letters?"

"No. Not to me. Not to anyone, as far as I know. And

two days later she had fallen down the stairs and was dead."

"Fallen down the stairs? Are you sure she did fall?"

"What do you mean?"

"She could have been pushed."

"Pushed?" Eulalie Vance looked at her blankly. "Pushed—what do you mean?"

It is easy to tell when someone theatrical has stopped acting, and Mrs. Pargeter could see that Eulalie Vance had just stopped. Her reaction was genuine surprise. The thought that Mrs. Selsby might have been murdered had never occurred to her.

Another name was struck off the list of suspects.

Mrs. Pargeter comforted her. Mrs. Selsby had been so vague and sleepy that she would never have noticed the absence of her letters. Anyway, by then she had been too short-sighted to read them. No, Eulalie shouldn't worry. It was something she had done in a fit of passion, but it had been an action with no unpleasant consequences for anyone.

At the end of this reassurance, Eulalie Vance rose. "Thank you for saying that. It makes me feel a lot better."

Mrs. Pargeter reflected that it wasn't what *she* had said that had made Eulalie feel better; it had just been the talking. Having made the mistake of showing an interest once, Mrs. Pargeter realised that she might be letting herself in for a whole lot more confidences about the actress's purple past.

"I'm going out for a walk, Melita. Clear my head."

"Good idea."

"Oh, I found this on the chair." She held out the diary. "Could you give it back?"

"Whose is it?" asked Mrs. Pargeter.

"Well, this is Mr. Dawlish's chair. I assume it's his."

41

12 MARCH—1:45 p.m.—*I am losing control. This is ridiculous. After last night's failure with the cyanide, I have now committed the total idiocy of leaving this diary around the hotel!*

Just a couple of days ago I felt so confident, and now I am in a state of trembling agitation like a schoolboy outside the headmaster's study. I must get a grip on myself, and recapture that coolness and detachment with which I planned and executed my two murders. I must not give way to morbid doubts.

God knows what I have unleashed by my carelessness with this book. I sat at lunch looking round the room, wondering who had handled it, and—worse—who read it. That snooper, Mrs. Pargeter, certainly had it, and, I don't doubt, read every

203

word. Then that idiot Eulalie Vance had her paws on it, too. Maybe even others, closer to me, have also looked inside.

The trouble is, this opens everything up so. Until my stupidity of leaving the book around, I thought that all I had to do to feel safe was to get rid of Mrs. Pargeter—now I won't feel secure until I've disposed of everyone living under the roof of the Devereux. Any one of them might have read this and be able to incriminate me.

At least I won't be caught that way again. I'll never let this book out of my sight—keep it in my pocket at all times in future.

I must keep calm. Take things one at a time. So far no one else has said anything to me. So far the only person I know to be a threat to me is that busybody, Mrs. Pargeter. I must get rid of her as soon as possible, and then I can assess calmly whether or not I have to murder anyone else.

I will watch her every movement. If she leaves the hotel at any time of the day or night, I will follow her. And this time I will not make any mistakes!

42

Mrs. Pargeter decided that the time had come for decisive action. She had done enough abstract, intellectual investigation; the moment had arrived to draw the murderer out of hiding and confront him.

The annoying thing was she didn't yet know who he was. She had narrowed the candidates down to the two men, but she could not yet be positive which of them had committed the murders.

She had seen both round lunchtime. Colonel Wicksteed, referring to a slight brightening of the weather, had observed that it was about time "the dogs of spring were let off their winter traces."

And Mr. Dawlish, to whom she had presented the diary just before lunch, had given her a most peculiar, abstracted, surprised look.

Of course she hadn't read any of the diary. She hadn't even opened it. This was another legacy of her life with the late Mr. Pargeter. He had kept a diary, but had always discouraged her from reading it. "It's not that there's anything in it I'm ashamed of, Melita my love," he always used to say. "It's just that what you don't know, you can't be made to stand up in court and say."

Mrs. Pargeter could respect the wisdom of that. Although there had been a temptation to read the diary that she had returned to Mr. Dawlish, to see if it contained anything that might be relevant to her investigation, it was a temptation she had resisted.

But the need for decisive action was strong. She felt the pressure and she knew that the murderer was feeling the pressure, too. The attempt to poison her had failed, but another attempt on her life must follow soon.

This time, however, she would be expecting the attack. That would give her the edge, and she reckoned she had a reasonable chance of turning the tables on him.

In her bedroom after lunch she had a little nap and then started to make her preparations.

She stowed the late Mr. Pargeter's small binoculars in her handbag, and then hesitated. Should she or shouldn't she?

The late Mr. Pargeter had not been a man of violence, although he had recognised the occasional necessity for it in a world depressingly lacking in moral standards. His attitude to violence was very similar to his attitude to the question of bringing in the police: Don't do it unless there really is no alternative.

Mrs. Pargeter tried to decide whether her late husband would have thought there was any alternative in her current situation.

She came to the conclusion that the late Mr. Pargeter's priority would be, as it had always been, that she should be well protected. And, while some husbands leave their widows only pensions, annuities and insurance policies, the late Mr. Pargeter had ensured that his should also have more practical means of protection.

She took the gun out of its secret compartment in the bottom of her suitcase. It was of American manufacture, a neat little weapon with a three-inch barrel, ideal for a lady's handbag. She slipped it in with the binoculars and put on her boots and mink coat.

She knew the risk she was taking, but she had got to the point where she had to find out the solution.

And she knew that whoever followed her out when she left the hotel would be the murderer of Mrs. Selsby and Mrs. Mendlingham.

She went into the Seaview Lounge and found all the surviving residents of the Devereux sitting there. Lady Ridgleigh was reading *Country Life*, Miss Wardstone *The Church Times*, and Eulalie Vance *The Stage*. In the bay window Colonel Wicksteed was looking out to sea with his binoculars.

"Japanese job out there," he pronounced.

"Ah," said Mr. Dawlish.

"Tanker. Make a lot of tankers, the Japs."

"Oh."

"Why there are so many problems in the Scottish shipyards, you know."

"Oh, really?" said Mr. Dawlish.

This little conversational surge having come to its end, Mrs. Pargeter announced to the assembled company, "Just going out for a stroll. Won't be long."

They all nodded or waved acknowledgement of this information.

In spite of the brighter weather, by late afternoon there was a brisk March wind beating along the Littlehampton sea front. Mrs. Pargeter, who had decided her route in advance, started walking firmly along the Promenade towards the mouth of Arun, the route on which she had followed Mrs. Mendlingham less than a week before.

She went about two hundred yards before looking back, but there was no one hurrying after her from the Devereux.

She disciplined herself not to look back again until she reached the corner of the Smart's Amusements building. There was a fluttering inside her, a fluttering of fear, certainly, but a fluttering that also contained a strong element of excitement, and even glee. It was a familiar sensation, one that she had often felt during her eventful life with the late Mr. Pargeter.

It seemed a very long time before she reached Smart's Amusements, but once there she stopped and knelt down, apparently to make some adjustment to her right boot.

She looked back over her shoulder.

Yes, now she was being followed.

But it wasn't just one resident of the Devereux coming after her. There were two of them. One tall and straight, the other small and stooped.

Mr. Dawlish *and* Colonel Wicksteed.

43

The fact that there were two of them confused her. She had been convinced that only one would follow; she was not quite sure how to proceed.

Her plan for confrontation with the murderer had been to talk to him in the shelters where she had spoken to Mrs. Mendlingham. They combined both privacy and a degree of safety. She would be able to talk there in the confidence that there would be people in adjacent booths. Given the murderer's cautious approach to his other crimes, he was not going to risk killing her with witnessses to hand.

But now both Mr. Dawlish and Colonel Wicksteed were coming towards her, deep in conversation, the situation was different. The confrontation would not take place. The murderer had set out on his grim task, only to find that his friend had tagged along. He would have to delay his next murder attempt, and Mrs. Pargeter would have to delay her confrontation.

That being the case, Mrs. Pargeter couldn't see much point in waiting round in one of the shelters to talk to them. The only conversation she'd get would be their usual circuitous banter, and she didn't feel it was the moment for more of that.

So when she reached the shelter, she turned down on to the beach along the side of the Arun estuary. The sea was some way away. The tide, nearly at its lowest point, accelerated the rush of brown water in the river. It looked icy and evil as it swept past.

She was half-way down the beach, still walking alongside the torrent, when, for the first time, she thought of a conspiracy theory.

Suppose Mr. Dawlish and Colonel Wicksteed had committed the murders *together*.

Suppose between them they had eliminated Mrs. Selsby and Mrs. Mendlingham. And now, between them, they were coming to eliminate her.

She looked back up the beach, and saw something that chilled her like a sudden blast of cold air.

The two men had left the Promenade and were coming down the beach towards her. They were not running, but they moved quickly and purposefully, following her exact course along the side of the swollen river.

Mrs. Pargeter tried to speed up, but the sand got spongier the further she went down the beach, and snatched at her boots as they sank with each step.

She looked back. For a moment the two old men had stopped, just at the point where the old sea defence ended and there was only a low wooden fence between the sand and the river. Colonel Wicksteed's tweed hat bent close to Mr. Dawlish's grey cap. They were talking animatedly, as if making final plans.

She ran on, now trying to cut left, away from the river, away from the sea, back up towards the safety of the Promenade and the Devereux. The beach was empty, except for the three of them. Early darkness and a soggy mist combined to isolate them, cut them off from the rest of humanity.

Her boots dragged in the hungry sand. She thought she could hear the heavy pad of pursuing footsteps. Stifling a scream, she looked back.

What she saw was the last thing she had expected. She missed the moment of his launch, but was just in time to see the body of Colonel Wicksteed, with tweed hat detached and arms outstretched, in mid-air between the sand and the river.

For a long second he seemed frozen, as in a photograph. Then he vanished from her sight into the unseen turbulence below.

Immobile with shock, she looked at the small, thin figure of Mr. Dawlish, hardly fifty metres away. She waited for him to come towards her, and she felt that, when he did, she would have no will left to run, that she would just stand waiting, offering no resistance to his hypnotic advance.

It was a long, long moment. Mr. Dawlish did not stir. He stayed looking down at the river, into which his friend had just disappeared.

Then he turned up towards the Promenade, and walked slowly back to the Devereux.

44

It was a quarter to four when she got back to the hotel. There was no one in the Entrance Hall, and in the Seaview Lounge only Mr. Dawlish sat, in his customary armchair. The other residents must have gone to powder their noses before reassembling to await the arrival of Loxton's tea trolley.

Mr. Dawlish had removed his cap, but was still wearing his overcoat. In spite of this, the usual rug was drawn over his thin knees.

On Mr. Dawlish's lap lay the familiar dark blue diary.

Mrs. Pargeter undid her mink coat and sat opposite the old man.

"Presumably he had no chance?"

Mr. Dawlish shook his head. " 'Fraid not. Water's

212

very fast at that time of the tide. And very cold. Shock of that might have killed him before he drowned."

"So . . . the same person killed Mrs. Selsby . . . and Mrs. Mendlingham . . . and now Colonel Wicksteed . . ."

"Yes." He looked across at her. "I thought you seemed to be an intelligent woman, but I didn't realise you'd worked it all out. Congratulations."

"Thank you." There was a silence. Then she said softly, "Can I ask why?"

Mr. Dawlish sighed. He reached down to his lap and picked up the dark blue diary that lay there.

"I think this'll explain everything," he said, as he handed it across.

45

12 MARCH—2:30 p.m.—*The worst has happened. As I feared, now it is not only Mrs. Pargeter who knows my secret, but someone else as well. And that person is my dearest friend. He came and told me after lunch. He had read this book and he knew all about my murders. He was sorry for me, he said, but was quite firm that I should go to the police and confess. If I didn't, he said, he would.*

So now I am faced with a frightful dilemma. Either I give myself up, or I have to murder the one person left in the world who means anything to me. And still murder Mrs. Pargeter— and who knows how many others before I feel secure? I now begin to suffer that self-contempt and hopelessness that murderers are supposed to feel. The crime is one that at first gives you a sensation of power, of controlling events, but how briefly

214

that euphoria lasts! How quickly one realises that the crime itself is in control! How I wish I had never embarked on this course!

And yet when I started—such a comparatively short time ago—it all seemed to make such good sense. I was in such a corner over the gambling debts. I had borrowed on the strength of my pension and used every other resource I possessed. They were threatening all kinds of things, but what worried me most was the threat that they would tell Miss Naismith. I was well set up at the Devereux and I planned to stay here for the rest of my days. For someone like me to be branded publicly as the kind of bounder who doesn't pay his gambling debts would have been insupportable.

I was in pretty total despair about it, when by chance, in a private conversation with me, Mrs. Selsby let slip about the unusual provisions of her will. I'm afraid from that moment I considered murder as a way out of my difficulties, and once the idea had caught hold of me, it grew stronger and stronger, until it became an obsession. I had only one aim and that was to kill Mrs. Selsby.

But of course it didn't stop there. Mrs. Mendlingham had seen what had happened and came to me with a proposition— if she kept quiet, then I was to use my influence to prevent Miss Naismith from turning her out of the Devereux. Of course that was ridiculous. I had no influence with Miss Naismith, and I think, anyway, she had already made up her mind that Mrs. Mendlingham should go. So there was no security for me till the old woman was dead.

But then Mrs. Pargeter started meddling. I tried to kill her, using cyanide from a suicide ring I'd had made up during the War, but I failed. Never mind, I'll try again—or at least I think I will.

Because where all was certainty, now all is doubt. Now that I am faced with the prospect of having to kill a friend, the situation is so different. The two old women were near the end, anyway. Mrs. Pargeter seems a pleasant enough soul, but I do not know her well nor feel any particular loyalty to her. But to have to kill him—I don't know if I can bring myself to do it.

I will go out for a walk with him. That will be best. Talk to him—see if I can make him change his mind about going to the police. And, if he won't change his mind, then I'll have to try and kill him.

Or, if I can't bring myself to do that, perhaps I'll have to kill myself instead.

46

Mrs. Pargeter finished reading and looked up at Mr. Dawlish. From the wrinkles around his eyes tears flowed unchecked.

"So," said Mrs. Pargeter sadly, "he chose the second alternative."

"Yes," said Mr. Dawlish. "I pleaded with him not to, but he said there was no other way out. I'm afraid he always used to win our arguments. He said it'd be better all round if he went. 'It's a much, much better thing I'm doing than I've ever done before,' he said."

Misquoting to the last, reflected Mrs. Pargeter, as Mr. Dawlish went on, "And he asked me to give this diary to you. He said it'd explain everything. He said he hoped you'd agree that his death tied up all the loose ends and that there was no need to go to the police about any of it."

"No. No need at all," she said, mindful of the late Mr. Pargeter's views on that particular subject.

47

A month passed before Mrs. Pargeter finally made her decision.

The genteel surface of life at the Devereux Hotel had settled down again. There were three new residents, all of impeccable references (and all personally interviewed by Miss Naismith before being admitted). There was a former bank manager named Mr. Poulton. There was a retired airline pilot called Preston-Carstairs (a gratifyingly double-barrelled name, which Miss Naismith took great pleasure in using at every possible opportunity). And there was another aristocratic widow called Lady Jacobson. (The arrival of the latter caused intense annoyance to Lady Ridgleigh, whose only comfort was that, with a name like that, the newcomer must undoubtedly be Jewish.)

The new residents soon adapted to the little ways of the Devereux, as did Newth's replacement, a taciturn man called Mulligan, who was a "born-again" Christian and served behind the Schooner Bar with the distaste that only a total abstainer can demonstrate. He did almost everything that Newth had done (except, fortunately, stealing jewels). He did not, however, serve Miss Naismith glasses of "Perrier" and she had to resort in the early evenings to the bottle of Gordon's in her bedroom. Nor did Miss Naismith send Mulligan on little missions to the video shop for her. She was now faced with the choice of either collecting her soft porn herself or not having any. Gentility won out and she gave up her little hobby.

The surviving residents did not change a lot. They remained "active." Eulalie Vance cornered each of the new arrivals in turn and treated them to tales of her passionate past. Miss Wardstone sniffed disapprovingly at everything and looked set to enjoy the life she so despised for another thirty years. Lady Ridgleigh still gave far too much of her dwindling resources to her worthless son.

The only one who changed, really, was Mr. Dawlish. Since his friend's death he seemed to have got smaller. He still spent much of his time in the bay window, looking out at the dismal sea, but, without Colonel Wicksteed's commentary, his interest in what he saw had gone. Like Mrs. Selsby before him, he seemed visibly to be fading, becoming more and more transparent. He remained fit, but no one would have been surprised to find that one morning he had simply evaporated into death.

It was at one of those moments just before Loxton came in with the tea trolley, that Mrs. Pargeter made her decision. It had been coming, she knew, for some time, but at that moment she was certain.

She looked around at the other residents, and she realised again what they all had in common. They didn't look forward; they looked backwards. They had all finished their lives. They had all come to the Devereux to spiral down to a genteel death.

And that was where the late Mr. Pargeter's widow differed from them. She still had a lot to look forward to.

No, she thought, as she rose from her armchair and went to tell Miss Naismith she would soon be leaving the Devereux, I'm not finished yet.

YOU'LL BE MAD FOR THESE MYSTERIES BY

Simon BRETT

Set in the sophisticated world of British theater, they star amateur sleuth, Charles Paris.

_____ DEAD GIVEAWAY	11914-6	$3.50
_____ DEAD ROMANTIC	20043-1	3.50
_____ SHOCK TO THE SYSTEM	18200-X	3.50
_____ SO MUCH BLOOD	18069-4	3.50
_____ STAR TRAP	18300-6	3.50
_____ TICKLED TO DEATH	18541-6	3.50

At your local bookstore or use this handy coupon for ordering:

DELL READERS SERVICE, DEPT. DSB, P.O. Box 5057, Des Plaines, IL. 60017-5057

Please send me the above title(s). I am enclosing $_____. (Please add $2.00 per order to cover shipping and handling.) Send check or money order—no cash or C.O.D.s please.

Ms./Mrs./Mr. _____

Address _____

City/State _____ Zip _____

DSB-11/88

Prices and availability subject to change without notice. Please allow four to six weeks for delivery. This offer expires 5/89.

Match wits with the best-selling

MYSTERY WRITERS

in the business!

ROBERT BARNARD
"A new grandmaster."—*The New York Times*
___CORPSE IN A GILDED GAGE   11465-9 $3.50
___OUT OF THE BLACKOUT   16761-2 $3.50

SIMON BRETT
"He's bloody marvelous!"—*Chicago Sun Times*
___DEAD GIVEAWAY   11914-6 $3.50
___SHOCK TO THE SYSTEM   18200-X $3.50

MARTHA GRIMES
"A writer to relish."—*The New Yorker*
___THE DIRTY DUCK   12050-0 $4.50
___I AM THE ONLY RUNNING
    FOOTMAN   13924-4 $4.50

SISTER CAROL ANNE O'MARIE
"Move over Miss Marple..."—*San Francisco Sunday Examiner & Chronicle*
___ADVENT OF DYING   10052-6 $3.50

JONATHAN VALIN
"A superior writer...smart and sophisticated."
      —*The New York Times Book Review*
___LIFE'S WORK   14790-5 $3.50

At your local bookstore or use this handy coupon for ordering:

DELL READERS SERVICE, DEPT. DGM
P.O. Box 5057, Des Plaines, IL. 60017-5057
Please send me the above title(s). I am enclosing $_____.
(Please add $2.00 per order to cover shipping and handling.) Send
check or money order—no cash or C.O.D.s please.

Ms./Mrs./Mr._____

Address _____

City/State _____ Zip _____

DGM-11/88
Prices and availability subject to change without notice. Please allow four to six
weeks for delivery. This offer expires 5/89.